THE CASINO
MURDER CASE

THE CASINO MURDER CASE

A PHILO VANCE MYSTERY

S. S. VAN DINE

Quam saepe forte temere eveniunt, quae
non audeas optare! —*Terence*.

CHARLES SCRIBNER'S SONS
NEW YORK

Special thanks to Ellen FitzSimons and Carol Brener for
their help with this edition.

First Charles Scribner's Sons paperback edition published
1985.

Published simultaneously in Canada by Collier Macmillan
Canada, Inc.—Copyright under the Berne Convention.

1 3 5 7 9 11 13 15 17 19 K/P 20 18 16 14 12 10 8 6 4 2

Printed in the United States of America.

ISBN 0-684-18503-2

TO
AUGUSTA MacMANNUS
("Our Mac")

CONTENTS

CHARACTERS OF THE BOOK

PHILO VANCE

JOHN F.-X. MARKHAM
District Attorney of New York County.

ERNEST HEATH
Sergeant of the Homicide Bureau.

MRS. ANTHONY LLEWELLYN
A prominent social worker.

RICHARD KINKAID
Her brother, and owner of the Casino.

AMELIA LLEWELLYN
Her daughter; an art student.

LYNN LLEWELLYN
Her son, a night-club habitué and gambler.

VIRGINIA LLEWELLYN
Lynn Llewellyn's wife: formerly Virginia Vale,
a musical-comedy star.

MORGAN BLOODGOOD
Former instructor in mathematics, and Kinkaid's chief croupier.

DOCTOR ALLAN KANE
A young doctor; friend of the Llewellyns.

DOCTOR ROGERS
A physician.

DOCTOR ADOLPH HILDEBRANDT
    Official Toxicologist.

SMITH
    The Llewellyn butler.

HENNESSEY
    Detective of the Homicide Bureau.

SNITKIN
    Detective of the Homicide Bureau.

SULLIVAN
    Detective of the Homicide Bureau.

BURKE
    Detective of the Homicide Bureau.

DOCTOR EMANUEL DOREMUS
    Medical Examiner.

CURRIE
    Vance's valet.

THE CASINO
MURDER CASE

CHAPTER I

(Saturday, October 15; 10 a. m.)

It was in the cold bleak autumn following the spectacular Dragon murder case* that Philo Vance was confronted with what was probably the subtlest and most diabolical criminal problem of his career. Unlike his other cases, this mystery was one of poisoning. But it was not an ordinary poisoning case: it involved far too clever a technique, and was thought out to far too many decimal points, to be ranked with even such famous crimes as the Cordelia Botkin, Molineux, Maybrick, Buchanan, Bowers and Carlyle Harris cases.

The designation given to it by the newspapers—namely, the Casino murder case—was technically a misnomer, although Kinkaid's famous gambling Casino in West 73rd Street played a large part in it. In fact, the first sinister episode in this notorious crime actually occurred beside the high-stake roulette table in the "Gold Room" of the Casino; and the final episode of the tragedy was enacted in Kin-

* "The Dragon Murder Case" (Scribners, 1933).

kaid's walnut-paneled Jacobean office, just off the main gambling salon.

Incidentally, I may say that that last terrible scene will haunt me to my dying day and send cold shivers racing up and down my spine whenever I let my mind dwell on its terrifying details. I have been through many shocking and unnerving situations with Vance during the course of his criminal investigations, but never have I experienced one that affected me as did that terrific and fatal dénouement that came so suddenly, so unexpectedly, in the gaudy environment of that famous gambling rendezvous.

And Markham, too, I know, underwent some chilling metamorphosis in those few agonizing moments when the murderer stood before us and cackled in triumph. To this day, the mere mention of the incident makes Markham irritable and nervous—a fact which, considering his usual calm, indicates clearly how deep and lasting an impression the tragic affair made upon him.

The Casino murder case, barring that one fatal terminating event, was not so spectacular in its details as many other criminal cases which Vance had probed and solved. From a purely objective point of view it might even have been considered commonplace; for in its superficial mechanism it had many parallels in well-known cases of criminological history. But what distinguished this case from its many antetypes was the subtle inner processes by which the murderer sought to divert suspicion and to create new and more devilish situations wherein the real motive of the crime was to be found. It was not merely one wheel within another wheel: it was an elaborate and complicated piece of psychological machinery, the mechanism of which led on and on, almost indefinitely, to the most amazing—and erroneous—conclusions.

Indeed, the first move of the murderer was perhaps the most artful act of the entire profound scheme. It was a letter addressed to Vance thirty-six hours before the mechanism of the plot was put in direct operation. But, curiously enough, it was this supreme subtlety that, in the end, led to the recognition of the culprit. Perhaps this act of letter-writing was too subtle: perhaps it defeated its own purpose by calling mute attention to the mental processes of the murderer, and thereby gave Vance an intellectual clue which fortunately diverted his efforts from the more insistent and more obvious lines of ratiocination. In any event, it achieved its superficial object; for Vance was actually a spectator of the first thrust, so to speak, of the villain's rapier.

And, as an eye witness to the first episode of this famous poison murder mystery, Vance became directly involved in the case; so that, in this instance, he carried the problem to John F.-X. Markham, who was then the District Attorney of New York County and Vance's closest friend; whereas, in all his other criminal investigations, it was Markham who had been primarily responsible for Vance's participation.

The letter of which I speak arrived in the morning mail on Saturday, October 15. It consisted of two typewritten pages, and the envelop was postmarked Closter, New Jersey. The official post-office stamp showed the mailing time as noon of the preceding day. Vance had worked late Friday night, tabulating and comparing the æsthetic designs on Sumerian pottery in an attempt to establish the cultural influences of this ancient civilization,* and did not arise till ten o'clock on Saturday. I was living in Vance's apartment in East 38th Street at the time; and though my position was that of legal adviser and monetary steward I had, during the past three years, gradually taken over a kind of general secretaryship in his employ. "Employ" is perhaps not the correct word, for Vance and I had been close friends since our Harvard days; and it was this relationship that had induced me to sever my connection with my father's law firm of Van Dine, Davis and Van Dine

---

* The records of the Joint Expedition to Mesopotamia, undertaken by the University of Pennsylvania and the British Museum, under the directorship of Doctor C. Leonard Woolley, had recently appeared.

and to devote myself to the more congenial task of looking after Vance's affairs.

On that raw, almost wintry, morning in October I had, as usual, opened and segregated his mail, taking care of such items as came under my own jurisdiction, and was engaged in making out his entry blanks for the autumn field trials,* when Vance entered the library and, with a nod of greeting, sat down in his favorite Queen-Anne chair before the open fire.

That morning he was wearing a rare old mandarin robe and Chinese sandals, and I was somewhat astonished at his costume, for he rarely came to breakfast (which invariably consisted of a cup of Turkish coffee and one of his beloved *Régie* cigarettes) in such elaborate dress.

"I say, Van," he remarked, when he had pushed the table-button for Currie, his aged English butler and majordomo; "don't look so naïvely amazed. I felt depressed when I awoke. I couldn't trace the designs on some of the jolly old stelæ and cylinder seals they've dug up at Ur, and in consequence had a restless night. Therefore, I bedecked myself in this Chinese attire in an effort to counteract my feelin's, and in the hope, I may add, that I would, through a

---

* Vance owned some exceptionally fine pointers and setters which had made many notable wins for him in the various trials in the East. They had been trained by one of the country's leading experts, and returned to Vance perfectly broken to field work. Vance took great pleasure in handling the dogs himself.

process of psychic osmosis, acquire a bit of that Oriental calm that is so highly spoken of by the Sinologists."

At this moment Currie brought in the coffee. Vance, after lighting a *Régie* and taking a few sips of the thick black liquid, looked toward me lazily and drawled: "Any cheerin' mail?"

So interested had I been in the strange anonymous letter which had just arrived—although I had as yet no idea of its tragic significance—that I handed it to him without a word. He glanced at it with slightly raised eyebrows, let his gaze rest for a moment on the enigmatic signature, and then, placing his coffee cup on the table, read it through slowly. I watched him closely during the process, and noted a curiously veiled expression in his eyes, which deepened and became unusually serious as he came to the end.

The letter is still in Vance's files, and I am quoting it here verbatim, for in it Vance found one of his most valuable clues—a clue which, though it did not actually lead to the murderer at the beginning, at least shunted Vance from the obvious line of research intended by the plotter. As I have just said, the letter was typewritten; but the work was inexpertly done—that is, there was evidence of the writer's unfamiliarity with the mechanism of a typewriter. The letter read:

DEAR MR. VANCE: I am appealing to you for help in my distress. And I am also appealing to you in the name of humanity and justice. I know you by reputation—and you are the one man in New York who may be able to prevent a terrible catastrophe—or at least to see that punishment is meted out to the perpetrator of an impending crime. Horrible black clouds are hovering over a certain household in New York —they have been gathering for years—and I *know* that the storm is about to break. There is danger and tragedy in the air. *Please* do not fail me at this time, although I admit I am a stranger to you.

I do not know exactly what is going to happen. If I did I could go to the police. But any official interference now would put the plotter on guard and merely postpone the tragedy. I wish I could tell you more—but I do not know any more. The thing is all frightfully vague— it is like an atmosphere rather than a specific situation. *But it is going to happen—something* is going to happen—and whatever does happen will be deceptive and untrue. So please don't let appearances deceive you. Look—*look* —*beneath* the thing for the truth. All those involved are abnormal and tricky. *Don't underestimate them.*

Here is all I can tell you——

You have met young Lynn Llewellyn—that much I know—and you probably know of his marriage three years ago to the beautiful musical-comedy star, Virginia Vale. She gave up her career and she and Lynn have been living with his family. But the marriage was a terrible mistake, and for three years a tragedy has been brewing. And now things have come to a climax. *I have seen the terrible forms taking shape.* And there are others besides the Llewellyns in the picture.

There is danger—*awful danger*—for some one—I don't know just who. *And the time is tomorrow night*, Saturday.

Lynn Llewellyn *must be watched*. And watched carefully.

There is to be a dinner at the Llewellyn home tomorrow night—and every principal in this impending tragedy will be present—Richard Kinkaid, Morgan Bloodgood, young Lynn and his unhappy wife, and Lynn's sister Amelia, and his mother. The occasion is the mother's birthday.

Although I know that there will be a rumpus of some kind at that dinner, I realize that you can do nothing about it. It will not matter anyway. The dinner will be only the beginning of things. But something momentous will happen *later. I know* it will happen. *The time has now come.*

After dinner Lynn Llewellyn will go to Kinkaid's Casino to play. He goes every Saturday night. I know that you yourself often visit the Casino. And what I beg of you to do is to go there tomorrow night. You *must* go. And you must watch Lynn Llewellyn—every minute of the time. Also watch Kinkaid and Bloodgood.

You may wonder why I do not take some action in the matter myself; but I assure you my position and the circumstances make it utterly impossible.

I wish I could be more definite. But I do not know any more to tell you. *You* must find out.

The signature, also typewritten, was "One Deeply Concerned."

When Vance had perused the letter a second time he settled deep in his chair and stretched his legs out lazily.

"An amazin' document, Van," he drawled, after several meditative puffs on his cigarette. "And quite insincere, don't y' know. A literary touch here and there—a bit of melodrama—a few samples of gaudy rhetoric—and, occasionally, a deep concern. . . . Quite, oh, quite: the signature, though vague, is genuine. Yes . . . yes—that's quite obvious. It's more heavily typed than the rest of the letter—more pressure on the keys. . . . Passion at work. And not a pleasant passion: a bit of vindictiveness, as it were, coupled with anxiety. . . ." His voice trailed off. "Anxiety!" he continued, as if to himself. "That's exactly what exudes from between the lines. But anxiety about what? about whom? . . . The gambling Lynn? It might be, of course. And yet . . ." Again his voice trailed off, and once more he inspected the letter, adjusting his monocle carefully and scrutinizing both sides of the paper. "The ordin'ry commercial bond," he observed. "Available at any stationer's. . . . And a plain envelop with a pointed flap. My anxious and garrulous correspondent was most careful to avoid the possibility of being traced through his stationer. . . . Very sad. . . . But I do wish the epistler had gone to business school at some time. The typing is atrocious: bad spacings, wrong keys struck, no sense of margin or indentation—all indicative of too little familiarity with the endless silly gadgets of the typewriter."

He lighted another cigarette and finished his coffee. Then he settled back in his chair and read the letter for the third time. I had seldom seen him so interested. At length he said:

"Why all the domestic details of the Llewellyns, Van? Any one who reads the newspapers knows of the situation in the Llewellyn home. The pretty blond actress marrying into the Social Register over the protests of mama and then ending up under mama's roof: Lynn Llewellyn a young gadabout and the darling of the night-clubs: serious little sister turning from the frivolities of the social whirl to study art:—who in this fair bailiwick could have failed to hear of these things? And mama herself is a noisy philanthropist and a committee member of every social and economic organization she can find. And certainly Kinkaid, the old lady's brother, is not an *inconnu*. There are few characters in the city more notorious than he—much to old Mrs. Llewellyn's chagrin and humiliation. The wealth of the family alone would make its doings common gossip." Vance made a wry face. "And yet my correspondent reminds me of these various matters. Why? Why the letter at all? Why am I chosen as the recipient? Why the flowery language? Why the abominable typing? Why this paper and the secrecy? Why everything? . . . I wonder . . . I wonder. . . ."

He rose and paced up and down. I was surprised at his perturbation: it was altogether unlike him. The letter had not impressed me very much, aside from its unusualness; and my first inclination was to regard it as the act of a crank or of some one who had a grudge against the Llewellyns and was taking this circuitous means of causing them annoyance. But Vance evidently had sensed something in the letter that had completely escaped me.

Suddenly he ceased his contemplative to-and-fro, and walked to the telephone. A few moments later he was speaking with District Attorney Markham, urging him to stop in at the apartment that afternoon.

"It's really quite important," he said, with but a trace of the usual jocular manner he assumed when speaking to Markham. "I have a fascinatin' document to show you. . . . Toddle up—there's a good fellow."

For some time after he had replaced the receiver

Vance sat in silence. Finally he rose and turned to the section of his library devoted to psychoanalysis and abnormal psychology. He ran through the indices of several books by Freud, Jung, Stekel and Ferenczi; and, marking several pages, he sat down again to peruse the volumes. After an hour or so he replaced the books on the shelves, and spent another thirty minutes consulting various reference books, such as "Who's Who," the New York "Social Register" and "The American Biographical Dictionary." Finally he shrugged his shoulders slightly, yawned mildly and settled himself at his desk, on which were spread numerous reproductions of the art works unearthed in Doctor Woolley's seven years' excavations at Ur.

Saturday being a half-day at the District Attorney's office, Markham arrived shortly after two o'clock. Vance meanwhile had dressed and had his luncheon, and he received Markham in the library.

"A sear and yellow day," he complained, leading Markham to a chair before the fireplace. "Not good for man to be alone. Depression rides me like a hag. I missed the field trial on Long Island today. Preferred to stay in and hover over the glowin' embers. Maybe I'm getting old and full of dreams. . . . Distressin'. . . . But I'm awfully grateful and all that for your comin'. How about a pony of 1811 *Napoléon* to counteract your autumnal sorrows?"

"I've no sorrows today, autumnal or otherwise," Markham returned, studying Vance closely. "And when you babble most you're thinking hardest—the unmistakable symptom." (He still scrutinized Vance.) "I'll take the cognac, however. But why the air of mystery over the phone?"

"My dear Markham—oh, my dear Markham! Really, now, was it an air of mystery? The melancholy days——"

"Come, come, Vance." Markham was beginning to grow restless. "Where's that interesting paper you wished me to see?"

"Ah, yes—quite." Vance reached into his pocket, and, taking out the anonymous letter he had received that morning, handed it to Markham. "It really should not have come on a depressin' day like this."

Markham read the letter through casually and then tossed it on the table with a slight gesture of irritation.

"Well, what of it?" he asked, attempting, without success, to hide his annoyance. "I sincerely hope you're not taking this seriously."

"Neither seriously nor frivolously," Vance sighed; "but with an open mind, old dear The epistle has possibilities, don't y' know."

"For Heaven's sake, Vance!" Markham protested. "We get letters like that every day. Scores of them. If we paid any attention to them we'd have time for nothing else. The letter-writing habit of professional trouble-makers—— But I don't have to go into that with you: you're too good a psychologist."

Vance nodded with unwonted seriousness.

"Yes, yes—of course. The epistol'ry complex. A combination of futile egomania, cowardice and Sadism—I'm familiar with the formula. But, really, y' know, I'm not convinced that this particular letter falls in that categ'ry."

Markham glanced up.

"You really think it's an honest expression of concern based on inside knowledge?"

"Oh, no. On the contr'ry." Vance regarded his cigarette meditatively. "It goes deeper than that. If it were a sincere letter it would be less verbose and more to the point. Its very verbosity and its stilted phraseology indicate an ulterior motive: there's too much thought behind it. . . . And there are sinister implications in it—an atmosphere of abnormal reasoning—a genuine note of cruel tragedy, as if a fiend of some kind were plotting and chuckling at the same time. . . . I don't like it, Markham—I don't at all like it."

Markham regarded Vance with considerable surprise. He started to say something, but, instead, picked up the letter and read it again, more carefully this time. When he had finished he shook his head slowly.

"No, Vance," he protested mildly. "The saddest days of the year have affected your imagination. This letter is merely the outburst of some hysterical woman similarly affected."

"There *are* a few somewhat feminine touches in it —eh, what?" Vance spoke languidly. "I noticed that. But the general tone of the letter is not one that points to hallucinations."

Markham waved his hand in a deprecatory gesture and drew on his cigar a while in silence. At length he asked:

"You know the Llewellyns personally?"

"I've met Lynn Llewellyn once—just a curs'ry introduction—and I've seen him at the Casino a number of times. The usual wild type of pampered darling whose mater holds the purse strings. And, of course, I know Kinkaid. Every one knows Richard Kinkaid but the police and the District Attorney's office." Vance shot Markham a waggish look. "But you're quite right in ignoring his existence and refusing to close his gilded den of sin. It's really run pretty straight, and only people who can afford it go there. My word! Imagine the naïveté of a mind that thinks gambling can be stopped by laws and raids! . . . The Casino is a delightful place, Markham—quite correct and all that sort of thing. You'd enjoy it immensely." Vance sighed dolefully. "If only you weren't the D. A.! Sad . . . sad. . . ."

Markham shifted uneasily in his chair, and gave Vance a withering look followed by an indulgent smile.

"I may go there some time—after the next election perhaps," he returned. "Do you know any of the others mentioned in the letter?"

"Only Morgan Bloodgood," Vance told him. "He's Kinkaid's chief croupier—his right hand, so to speak. I know him only professionally, however, though I've heard he's a friend of the Llewellyns and knew Lynn's wife when she was in musical comedy. He's a college man, a genius at figures: he majored in mathematics at Princeton, Kinkaid told me once. Held an instructorship for a year or two, and then threw in his lot with Kinkaid. Probably needed excitement—anything's preferable to the quantum theory. . . . The other prospective *dramatis personæ* are unknown to me. I never even saw Virginia Vale—I was abroad during her brief triumph on the stage. And old Mrs. Llewellyn's path has never crossed mine. Nor have I ever met the art-aspiring daughter, Amelia."

"What of the relations between Kinkaid and old Mrs. Llewellyn? Do they get along as brother and sister should?"

Vance looked up at Markham languidly.

"I'd thought of that angle, too." He mused for a moment. "Of course, the old lady is ashamed of her wayward brother—it's quite annoyin' for a fanatical social worker to harbor a brother who's a professional gambler; and while they're outwardly civil to each other, I imagine there's internal friction, especially as the Park-Avenue house belongs to them jointly and they both live under its protectin' roof. But I don't think the old girl would carry her animosity so far as to do any plotting against Kinkaid. . . . No, no. We can't find an explanation for the letter along that line. . . ."

At this moment Currie entered the library.

"Pardon me, sir," he said to Vance in a troubled tone; "but there's a person on the telephone who wishes me to ask you if you intend to be at the Casino tonight——"

"Is it a man or a woman?" Vance interrupted.

"I—really, sir——" Currie stammered, "I couldn't say. The voice was very faint and indistinct—disguised, you might say. But the person asked me to tell you that he—or she, sir—would not say another word, but would wait on the wire for your answer."

Vance did not speak for several moments.

"I've rather been expecting something of the sort," he murmured finally. Then he turned to Currie. "Tell my ambiguously sexed caller that I will be there at ten o'clock."

Markham took his cigar slowly from his mouth and looked at Vance with troubled concern.

"You actually intend to go to the Casino because of that letter?"

Vance nodded seriously.

"Oh, yes—quite."

CHAPTER II

(Saturday, October 15; 10:30 p. m.)

Richard Kinkaid's famous old gambling establishment, the Casino, in West 73rd Street, near West End Avenue, had, in its heyday, many claims to the glories of the long-defunct Canfield's. It flourished but a short time, yet its memory is still fresh in many minds, and its fame has spread to all parts of the country. It forms a glowing and indispensable link in the chain of resorts that runs through the spectacular history of the night life of New York. A towering apartment house, with terraces and penthouses, now rises where the Casino once stood.

To the uninitiated passer-by the Casino was just another of those large and impressive gray-stone mansions which were once the pride of the upper West Side. The house had been built in the 'Nineties and was the residence of Richard's father, Amos Kinkaid (known as "Old Amos"), one of the city's shrewdest and wealthiest real-estate operators. This particular property was the one parcel that had been willed outright to Richard Kinkaid in Old Amos's will: all the other property had been bequeathed jointly to his two children, Kinkaid and Mrs. Anthony Llewellyn. Mrs. Llewellyn, at the time of the inheritance, was already a widow with two children, Lynn and Amelia, both in their early teens.

Richard Kinkaid had lived alone in the gray-stone house for several years after Old Amos's death. He had then locked its doors, boarded up its windows, and indulged his desire for travel and adventure in the remote places of the earth. He had always had an irresistible instinct for gambling—perhaps a heritage from his father—and in the course of his travels he had visited most of the famous gambling resorts of Europe. As you may recall, the accounts of his spectacular gains and losses often reached the front pages of this country's press. When his losses had far exceeded his gains Kinkaid returned to America, a poorer but no doubt a wiser man.

Counting on political influence and powerful personal connections, he then decided to make an endeavor to recoup his losses by opening a fashionable gambling house of his own, patterned along the lines of some of America's famous houses of the old days.

"The trouble with me," Kinkaid had told one of his chief under-cover supporters, "is that I've always gambled on the wrong side of the table."

He had the big house in 73rd Street remodelled and redecorated, furnished it with the most lavish appointments, and entered upon his notorious enterprise "on the right side of the table." These embellishments of the house, so rumor had it, all but exhausted the remainder of his patrimony. He named the new establishment Kinkaid's Casino, in cynical memory perhaps of Monte Carlo. But so well known did the place become among the social elect and the wealthy, that the prefix "Kinkaid's" soon became superfluous: there was only one "Casino" in America.

The Casino, like so many of the extra-legal establishments of its kind, and like the various fashionable night-clubs that sprang up during the prohibition era, was run as a private club. Membership was requisite, and all applicants were prudently investigated and weighed. The initiation fee was sufficiently high to discourage all undesirable elements; and the roster of those who were accorded the privileges of the "club" read almost like a compilation of the names of the socially and professionally prominent.

For his chief croupier and supervisor of the games, Kinkaid had chosen Morgan Bloodgood, a cultured young mathematician whom he had met at his sister's home. Bloodgood had been at college with Lynn Llewellyn, though the latter was his senior by three years; and, incidentally, it was Bloodgood who brought about the meeting of Virginia Vale and young Llewellyn. Bloodgood, while in college and during the time he had taught mathematics, had, as a hobby, busied himself with the laws of probability. He applied his findings especially to the relation of these laws to numerical gambling, and had figured out elaborately the percentages in all the well-known games of chance. His estimates of permutations, possibilities of repetitions and changes of sequence as bearing on card games are today officially used in computing chances in drawings; and he was at one time associated with the District Attorney's office in exposing the overwhelming chances in favor of the owners in connection with a city-wide campaign against slot-machines of all types.

Kinkaid was once asked why he had chosen young Bloodgood in preference to an old-time, experienced croupier; and he answered:

"I am like Balzac's old Gobseck, who gave all his personal legal business to the budding solicitor, Derville, on the theory that a man under thirty can be relied upon, but that after that age no man may be wholly trusted."

The assistant croupiers and dealers at the Casino were likewise chosen from the ranks of well-bred, non-professional young men of good appearance and education; and they were carefully trained in the intricacies of their duties.*

Cynical though Kinkaid's philosophy may have

* It is interesting to note that this same method of selecting and training dealers has been followed at Agua Caliente.

been, the practical application of it met with success. His gambling from the "right side of the table" prospered. He was content with the usual house percentage, and the shrewdest of gamblers and experts were never able to bring against him an accusation of "fixing" any of his games.* In all disputes between a player and the croupier, the player was paid without question. Many small fortunes were lost and won at the Casino during its comparatively brief existence; and the play was always large, especially on Friday and Saturday nights.

When Vance and I arrived at the Casino on that fatal Saturday night of October 15, there was as yet only a scattering of guests present. It was too early for the full quota of habitués who, as a rule, came after the theatre.

As we walked up the wide stone steps from the paved outer court and entered the narrow vestibule of plate glass and black ironwork, we were greeted with a nod from a Chinese porter who stood at the left of the entrance. By some secret signal our identity was communicated to those in charge on the inside; and almost simultaneously with our arrival in the vestibule the great bronze door (which Old Amos had brought over from Italy) was swung open. In the spacious reception hall, fully thirty feet square,

---

* Kinkaid even employed the European roulette wheels with only the single "O".

hung with rich brocades and old paintings, and furnished in luxurious Italian Renaissance style, our hats and coats were taken from us by two uniformed attendants, both of them extremely tall and powerful men.*

At the rear of the hall was a divided marble stairway which led, on either side of a small glistening fountain, to the gaming rooms above.

On the second floor Kinkaid had combined the former drawing-room and the reception-room into one large salon which he had christened the Gold Room. It ran the entire width of the house and was perhaps sixty feet long. The west wall was broken by an alcove which was furnished as a small lounge. The salon was decorated in modified Roman style, with an occasional suggestion of Byzantine ornamentation. The walls were covered with gold leaf, and the flat marble pilasters, which broke them into large rectangular panels, were of a subdued ivory tone that blended with the gold of the walls and the buff-colored ceiling. The draperies at the long windows were of yellow silk brocaded with gold; and the deep-piled carpet was a neutralized ochre in color.

There were three roulette tables set down the centre of the room, two black-jack, or *vingt-et-un*, tables at the middle of the east and west walls, four

---

* I imagine Kinkaid got his idea for these enormous attendants from the impressive giants in the entrance-hall of the Savoy dining-room in London.

chuck-a-luck tables, or bird cages, in the four corners, and an elaborate dice table at the far end, between the windows. At the rear of the Gold Room, to the west, was a private card room, with a row of small individual tables where any form of solitaire could be played, and a dealer to look on and to pay or collect, according to the luck and skill of the player. Adjoining this room, to the east, was a crystal bar with a wide archway leading into the main salon. Here only the finest liquors and wines were served. These two rooms had evidently been the main dining-room and the breakfast room of the old Kinkaid mansion. A cashier's cage had been constructed in what had once been a linen closet, to the left of the bar.

Richard Kinkaid's private office had been constructed by shutting off the front end of the upper hallway. It had one door leading into the bar and another into the Gold Room. This office was about ten feet square and was paneled in walnut—a sombre yet beautifully appointed room, with a single frosted-glass window opening on the front court.

(I mention the office here because it played so important a part in the final terrible climax of the tragedy that was soon to begin before our eyes.)

When, that Saturday night, we had reached the narrow hall on the second floor, that led, through a wide draped entrance, into the main salon, Vance glanced casually into the two playing rooms and then turned into the bar.

"I think, Van, we'll have ample time for a sip of champagne," he said, with a curious restraint in his voice. "Our young friend is sitting in the lounge, quite by himself, apparently absorbed in computations. Lynn is a system player; and all manner of prelimin'ries are necess'ry before he can begin. If anything untoward is going to befall him tonight, he is either blissfully unaware of it or serenely indifferent. However, there's no one in the room now who could reasonably be interested in his existence—or his non-existence, for that matter—so we might as well bide a wee in here."

He ordered a bottle of 1904 *Krug*, and settled back, with outward placidity, in the sprawling chair beside the little table on which the wine was served. But, despite his apparently languid manner, I knew that some unusual tension had taken hold of him: this was obvious to me from the slow, deliberate way in which he took his cigarette from his mouth and broke the ashes in the exact centre of the tray.

We had scarcely finished our champagne when Morgan Bloodgood, emerging from a rear door, passed through the bar toward the main salon. He was a tall, slight man with a high, somewhat bulging forehead, a thin straight aquiline nose, heavy, almost flabby, lips, a pointed chin, and prominent

Darwinian ears with abnormally large tragi and receding lobes. His eyes were hard and smouldering and of a peculiar gray-green cast; and they were so deeply sunken as to appear in almost perpetual shadow. His hair was thin and sand-colored; and his complexion was sallow to the point of bloodlessness. Yet he was not an unattractive man. There was coolness and calm in the ensemble of his features—an immobility that gave the impression of latent power and profound trains of thought. Though I knew he was barely thirty, he could easily have passed for a man of forty or more.

When he caught sight of Vance he paused and nodded with reserved pleasantry.

"Going to try your luck tonight, Mr. Vance?" he asked in a deep mild voice.

"By all means," Vance returned, smiling only with his lips. Then he added: "I have a new system, don't y' know."

"That's bully for the house," grinned Bloodgood. "Based on Laplace or von Kries?" (I thought I detected a suggestion of sarcasm in his voice.)

"Oh, my dear fellow!" Vance replied. "Really, now! I rarely go in for abstruse mathematics: I leave that branch of research to experts. I prefer Napoleon's simple maxim: '*Je m'engage et puis je vois.*'"

"That's as good—or as bad—as any other system," Bloodgood retorted. "They all amount to the same thing in the end." And with a stiff bow he passed on into the Gold Room.

Through the divided portières we saw him take his place at the wheel of the centre roulette table.

Vance put down his glass and, carefully lighting another *Régie*, rose leisurely.

"I opine the time to mingle has come," he murmured, as he moved toward the archway leading into the Gold Room.

As we entered the salon the door of Kinkaid's office opened, and Kinkaid appeared. On seeing Vance he smiled professionally, and greeted him in a tone of stereotyped geniality:

"Good evening, sir. You're quite a stranger here."

"Charmed not to have been entirely forgotten, don't y' know," Vance returned dulcetly. "Especially," he added, in a steady, flat voice, "as one of my objects in comin' tonight was to see you."

Kinkaid stiffened almost imperceptibly.

"Well, you see me, don't you?" he asked, with a cold smile and a simulated air of good-nature.

"Oh, quite." Vance, too, became facetiously cordial. "But I should infinitely prefer seein' you in the restful Jacobean surroundings of your private office."

Kinkaid looked at Vance with narrowed searching eyes. Vance returned the gaze steadily, without permitting the smile to fade from his lips.

Without a word Kinkaid turned and reopened the office door, stepping aside to let Vance and me precede him. He followed us, and closed the door behind him. Then he stood stiffly and, with steady eyes on Vance, waited.

Vance lifted his cigarette to his lips, took a deep inhalation, and blew a ribbon of smoke toward the ceiling.

"I say, might we sit down?" he asked casually.

"By all means—if you're tired." Kinkaid spoke in a metallic voice, his face an expressionless mask.

"Thanks awfully." Vance ignored the other's attitude, and settling himself in one of the low leather-covered chairs near the door, crossed his knees in lazy comfort.

Despite Kinkaid's unfriendly manner, I felt that the man was not at bottom antagonistic to his guest, but that, as a hardened gambler, he was assuming a defensive bearing in the face of some possible menace the nature of which was unknown to him. He knew, as every one else in the city knew, that Vance was closely, even though unofficially, associated with the District Attorney; and it occurred to me that Kinkaid probably thought Vance had come to him as proxy on some unpleasant official mission. His reaction to such a suspicion would naturally have been this belligerently guarded attitude.

Richard Kinkaid, his superficial appearance as

the conventional gambler notwithstanding, was a cultured and intelligent man. He had been an honor student at college, and held two academic degrees. He spoke several languages fluently and, in his younger days, had been an archæologist of considerable note. He had written two books on his travels in the Orient, both of which may be found today in every public library.

He was a large man, nearly six feet tall; and despite his tendency to corpulency, it was obvious that he was powerfully built. His iron-gray hair, cut in a short pompadour, looked very light in contrast with his ruddy complexion. His face was oval, but his coarse features gave him an aspect of ruggedness. His brow was low and broad; his nose short, flat and irregular; and his mouth was pinched and hard—a long, straight, immobile slit. His eyes, however, were the outstanding feature of his face. They were small, and the lids sloped downward at the outer corners, like those of a man with Bright's disease, so that the pupils seemed always to be above the centres of the visible orbs, giving to his expression a sardonic, almost sinister, cast. There were shrewdness, perseverance, subtlety, cruelty and aloofness in his eyes.

As he stood before us that night, one hand resting on the beautifully carved flat-top desk at the window, the other stuffed deep into the side pocket of his dinner jacket, he kept his gaze fixed on Vance, without displaying either annoyance or concern: his was the perfect "poker face."

"What I wished to see you about, Mr. Kinkaid," Vance remarked at length, "is a letter I received this morning. It occurred to me it might interest you, inasmuch as your name was not too fondly mentioned in it. In fact, it intimately concerns the various members of your family."

Kinkaid continued to gaze at Vance without change of expression. Nor did he speak or make the slightest move.

Vance contemplated the end of his cigarette for a moment. Then he said:

"I think it might be best if you perused this letter yourself."

He reached into his pocket and handed the two typewritten pages to Kinkaid, who took them indifferently and opened them.

I watched him closely as he read. No new expression appeared in his eyes, and his lips did not move; but the color of his face deepened perceptibly, and, when he had reached the end, the muscles in his cheeks were working spasmodically. His fat neck bulged over his collar, and ugly splotches of red spread over it.

The hand in which he held the letter dropped jerkily to his side, as if the muscles of his arm were tense; and he slowly lifted his gaze until it met Vance's eyes.

"Well, what about it?" he asked through his teeth.

Vance moved his hand in a slight negative gesture of rejection.

"I'm not placin' any bets just now," he said quietly. "I'm takin' them."

"And suppose I'm not betting?" retorted Kinkaid.

"Oh, that's quite all right." Vance smiled icily. "Every one's prerogative, don't y' know."

Kinkaid hesitated a moment; then he grunted deep in his throat and sat down in the chair before the desk, placing the letter before him. After a minute or so of silence he thumped the letter with his knuckles and shrugged.

"I'd say it was the work of some crank." His tone was at once light and contemptuous.

"No, no. Really, now, Mr. Kinkaid," Vance protested blandly. "That won't do—it won't at all do. You've chosen the wrong number, as it were. You lose that chip. Why not make another selection?"

"What the hell!" exploded Kinkaid. He swung round in the swivel chair and glared at Vance with cold, penetrating menace. "I'm no damned detective," he went on, his lips scarcely moving. "What has the letter to do with me, anyway?"

Vance did not reply. Instead he met Kinkaid's vindictive gaze with cool, steady calm—a calm at once impersonal and devastating. I have never envied any one the task of out-staring Vance. There was a subtle psychological power in his gaze, when he wished to exert it, that could not be resisted by the strongest natures that sought to oppose him through the projection of that inner character which is conveyed by the direct stare.

Kinkaid, with all his forcefulness of mind, had met his match. He knew that Vance's gaze would neither drop nor shift; and in that silent communication that takes place between two strong adversaries when they look deep into each other's eyes—that strange wordless duel of personalities—Kinkaid capitulated.

"Very well," he said, with a good-natured smile. "I'll place another wager—if that'll help you any." He glanced over the letter again. "There's a hell of a lot of truth here. Whoever wrote this knows something about the family situation."

"You use a typewriter yourself—eh, what?" asked Vance.

Kinkaid started and then forced a laugh.

"Just about as rotten as that," he returned, waving his hand toward the letter.

Vance nodded sympathetically.

"I'm no good at it myself," he remarked lightly, "Beastly invention, the typewriter. . . . But I say, do you think any one intends to harm young Llewel-lyn?"

"I don't know, but I hope so," Kinkaid snapped, with an ugly grin. "He needs killing."

"Why not do it yourself then?" Vance's tone was matter-of-fact.

Kinkaid chuckled unpleasantly.

"I've often thought of it. But he's hardly worth the risk."

"Still," mused Vance, "you seem more or less tolerant of your nephew in public."

"Family prejudice, I suppose," Kinkaid said. "The curse of nepotism. My sister dotes on him."

"He spends considerable time here at the Casino." The remark was half question, half statement.

Kinkaid nodded.

"Trying to annex some of the Kinkaid money which his mother won't supply him too freely. And I humor him. Why not? He plays a system." Kinkaid snorted. "I wish they'd all play a system. It's the hit-or-miss babies that cut down the profits."

Vance turned the conversation back to the letter.

"Do you believe," he asked, "that there's a tragedy hanging over your family?"

"Isn't there one hanging over every family?" Kinkaid returned. "But if anything's going to happen to Lynn I hope it doesn't happen in the Casino."

"At any rate," persisted Vance, "the letter insists that I come here tonight and watch the johnnie."

Kinkaid waved his hand.

"I'd discount that."

"But you just admitted that there is a lot of truth in the letter."

Kinkaid sat motionless for a while, his eyes, like two small shining disks, fixed on the wall. At length he leaned forward and looked squarely at Vance.

"I'll be frank with you, Mr. Vance," he said earnestly. "I've a hell of a good idea who wrote that letter. Simply a case of mania and cold feet. . . . Forget it."

"My word!" murmured Vance. "That's dashed interestin'." He crushed out his cigarette and, rising, picked up the letter, refolded it, and put it back into his pocket. "Sorry to have troubled you and all that. . . . I think, however, I'll loiter a bit."

Kinkaid neither rose nor said a word as we went out into the Gold Room.

CHAPTER III

(Saturday, October 15; 11:15 p. m.)

The place had already begun to fill. There were at least a hundred "members" playing at the various tables and standing chatting in small groups. There was a gala, colorful atmosphere in the great room, coupled with a tinge of excitement and tension. The Japanese orderlies, in native costume, were darting about noiselessly on their various errands; and on either side of the arched entrance stood two uniformed attendants. No movement, however innocent, of any person escaped the ever-watchful eyes of these sentinels. It was a fashionable gathering; and I had no difficulty in identifying many prominent persons from social and financial circles.

Lynn Llewellyn was still sitting in a corner of the lounge, busily engaged with pencil and note-book and apparently oblivious to all the activity going on about him.

Vance strolled down the length of the room, greeting a few acquaintances on his way. He paused at the chuck-a-luck table near the east front window and bought a stack of chips. These he wagered on the "one," doubling each time up to five, and then beginning again. It was incredible how many "ones" showed up on the dice in the cage; and after fifteen minutes Vance had won nearly a thousand dollars. He seemed restless, though, and took his winnings indifferently.

Turning again to the centre of the room he walked to the roulette table operated by Bloodgood. He looked on for several turns of the wheel from behind a chair, and then sat down to join the play. He was facing the lounge alcove, and as he took his place at the table he glanced casually in that direction and let his eyes rest for a moment on Llewellyn, who was still deep in thought.

The selections for the next turn of the wheel had been made,—there were only five or six players engaged at the time,—and Bloodgood stood with the ball poised against his middle finger in the trough of the bowl, ready to project it on its indeterminate convolutions. But for some reason he did not flip it at once.

"*Faites votre jeu, monsieur,*" he called in a facetious sing-song, looking directly at Vance.

Vance turned his head quickly and met the slightly cynical smile on Bloodgood's heavy lips.

"Thanks awfully for the personal signal," he said, with exaggerated graciousness; and, leaning far up the table toward the wheel, he placed a hundred-dollar bill on the green area marked "0" at the head of the three columns of figures. "My system tells me to play the 'house number' tonight."

The faint smile on Bloodgood's lips faded, and his eyebrows went up a trifle. Then he spun the wheel dexterously.

It was a long play, for the ball had been given a terrific impetus and it danced back and forth for some time between the grooved wheel and the sides of the bowl. At length it seemed to settle in one of the numbered compartments, though the wheel was still spinning too rapidly to permit the reading of the numerals; but it leaped out again, made one or two gyrations, and finally came to rest in the green slot—the "house number."

A hum went up round the table as the rake gathered in all the other stakes; but though I watched Bloodgood's face closely, I could not detect the slightest change of expression:—he was the perfect unemotional croupier.

"Your system seems to be working," he remarked to Vance, as he moved out a stack of thirty-five yellow chips. *"Vous vous engagez, et puis vous voyez. . . . Mais, qu'est-ce que vous espérez voir, monsieur?"*

"I haven't the groggiest notion," returned Vance, gathering up his bill and the chips. "I'm not hopin' —I'm driftin'."

"In any event, you're lucky tonight," smiled Bloodgood.

"I wonder. . . ." Vance slid his winnings into his pocket and turned from the table.

He walked slowly toward the card room, paused at the entrance, and then moved on to the *vingt-et-un* game which was in progress at a high semi-circular table only a few yards from the lounge alcove. There were two vacant chairs facing the hallway; but Vance waited. The dealer sat on a small raised platform, and when the player at his right relinquished his seat Vance took the vacant chair. I noted that from this position he had an unobstructed view of Llewellyn.

He placed a yellow chip on the paneled section of the table in front of him, and a closed card was dealt to him. He glanced at it: standing behind him, I saw that it was the ace of clubs. The next card dealt him was another ace.

"Fancy that, Van," he remarked to me over his shoulder. "The 'ones' are followin' me around tonight."

He turned up his first ace and laid the other beside it, placing another yellow chip on it. He was the last to be served by the dealer on the "draw"; and to my astonishment he drew two face cards—a knave and a queen. This combination of an ace and a face card constitutes a "natural"—the highest hand in black-jack—and Vance had drawn two of them on the one deal. The dealer's cards totalled nineteen.

Vance was about to wager a second hand when Llewellyn rose with determination from his seat in the corner of the lounge and approached Bloodgood's roulette table, with note-book in hand. Instead of continuing the play, Vance again took up his winnings, slid from his high chair, and sauntered back to the centre of the room, taking his place behind the row of chairs on the side of the roulette table opposite to that at which Llewellyn had seated himself.

Lynn Llewellyn was of medium height and slender, with a suggestion of quick wiry strength. His eyes were a flat, dull blue, and though they moved quickly, they showed no animation. His mouth, however, was emotional and mobile. His thin, somewhat haggard face gave one the impression of weakness coupled with cunning; yet withal it was a capable face—a face which a certain type of woman would consider handsome.

When he had taken his seat he looked about him swiftly, nodded to Bloodgood and to others present, but apparently did not see Vance, although Vance stood directly across the table. He watched the play for several minutes, making a notation of the winning numbers in the leather-bound booklet he had placed before him on the table. After five or six plays, he began to frown, and, turning in his chair, summoned one of the Japanese boys who was passing.

"Scotch," he ordered; "with plain water on the side."

While the drink was being fetched he continued his notations. At length, when three numbers in the same column had come in succession, he began eagerly to play. When the boy brought the Scotch he waved it brusquely away, and concentrated on the game.

For the first half-hour that we stood watching him I tried to trace some mathematical sequence in his choice of numbers, but, meeting with no success, I gave it up. I later learned that Llewellyn was playing a curious and, according to Vance, a wholly inconsistent and contradictory variation of the Labouchère—or, as it is popularly called, Labby—system which, for many years, was thoroughly tested at Monte Carlo.

But, however inadequate the system may have been scientifically, Llewellyn was profiting by it. Indeed, had he followed up his advantages, after the un-reasoned custom of the amateur player, he would, as it happened, have progressed more rapidly. But each time he caught a number *(en plein)* or a half-number *(à cheval)* or a quarter-number *(en carré)* he withdrew his winnings in proportion to their du-plication, multiplying only when luck went against him. After almost every play he glanced quickly at the carefully ruled tables and columns of figures in his book; and it was obvious that, despite all temptation to do otherwise, he was abiding rigidly by the set formula he had decided to follow.

Shortly after midnight, when one of his suites of doubling had reached its peak, the right number came. The result was a large winning, and when he had drawn down the six piles of yellow chips, he took a deep tremulous breath and leaned back in his chair. I calculated roughly that he was approximately ten thousand dollars ahead at this point. News of his luck soon spread to the other players in the room, and there was a general gathering of the curious around Bloodgood's table.

I glanced about me and noted the various expressions of the spectators: some were cynical, some envious, some merely interested. Bloodgood himself showed no indication, either by a look or an intonation of voice, that anything unusual was taking place. He was the faultless automaton, discharging his duties with detached mechanical precision.

When Llewellyn relaxed in his seat after this coup he glanced up, and, catching sight of Vance, bowed abstractedly. He was still busy with his calculations and computations, noting each turn of the wheel, and recording the winning number in his book. His face had become flushed, and his lips moved nervously as he jotted down the figures. His hands trembled perceptibly, and every few moments he took a long deep inhalation, as if trying to calm his nerves. Once or twice I noticed that he threw his left shoulder forward and bent his head to the left, like a man with angina pectoris trying to relieve the pain over his heart.

After the sixth play had passed, Llewellyn leaned over and continued his careful system of selecting and pyramiding. This time I noticed that he introduced some new variations into his method. He did what is known as "covering" his bets, by setting the even-money black and red fields against the color of the number he chose, and by opposing the *première*, *milieu*, or *dernière douzaine* against the particular group of twelve in which he had made his *en plein* numerical choice, as well as by utilizing both the odd and even fields (*pair* and *impair*), and the high and low field (*passe* and *manque*), in the same manner.

"That byplay," Vance whispered in my ear, "is not on the books. He's losing his nerve, and is toying with both the d'Alembert and the Montant Belge systems. But it really doesn't matter in the least. If he's lucky he'll win anyway; if he's not, he'll lose. Systems are for optimists and dreamers. The immutable fact remains that the house pays thirty-five to one against thirty-six possibilities and an added house number. That's destiny—no one can conquer it."

But Llewellyn's luck at roulette was evidently running in his favor that night, for it was but a short time before he won again on a pyramided number. When he drew the chips to him his hands shook so that he upset one of the stacks and had difficulty in reassembling it. Again he sank back in his chair and let the next plays pass. His color had deepened; his eyes took on an unnatural glitter; and the muscles of his face began to twitch. He gazed about him blankly and missed one of the numbers that had shown on the wheel, so that he had to ask Bloodgood for it in order to keep the entries in his book complete.

A tension had taken hold of the spectators. A strange lull replaced the general conversation. Every one seemed intent on the outcome of this age-old conflict between a man and the unfathomed laws of probability. Llewellyn sat there with a fortune in chips piled up in front of him. A few more thousand dollars and the bank would be "broken"; for Kinkaid had set a nightly capital of forty thousand dollars for this table.

During the electrified silence that had suddenly settled over the room, broken only by the whirr of the spinning ball, the clink of chips and the droning voice of Bloodgood, Kinkaid emerged from his office and approached the table. He halted beside Vance, and indifferently watched the play for a while.

"This is evidently Lynn's night," he remarked casually.

"Yes, yes—quite." Vance did not take his eyes from the nervous trembling figure of Llewellyn.

At this moment Llewellyn again caught an *en plein*, but he had only a single chip on the number. However, it marked the end of some mathematical cycle, according to his confused system; and, withdrawing his chips, he leaned back once more. He was breathing heavily, as if he could not get sufficient air into his lungs; and again he thrust his left shoulder forward.

A Japanese boy was passing, and Llewellyn hailed him.

"Scotch," he ordered again, and, with apparent effort, jotted down the winning number in his book.

"Has he been drinking much tonight?" Kinkaid asked Vance.

"He ordered one drink some time ago but didn't take it," Vance told him. "This will be his first, as far as I know."

A few minutes later the boy set down beside Llewellyn a small silver tray holding a glass of whisky, an empty glass and a small bottle of charged water. Bloodgood had just spun the wheel, and he glanced at the tray.

"Mori!" he called to the boy. "Mr. Llewellyn takes plain water."

The Japanese turned back, set the whisky on the table before Llewellyn, and, taking up the tray with the charged water, moved away. As he came round the end of the table, Kinkaid beckoned to him.

"You can get the plain water from my carafe in the office," he suggested.

The boy nodded and hastened on his errand.

"Lynn needs a drink in a hurry," Kinkaid remarked to Vance. "No use holding him up, with that crowd in the bar. . . . The damned fool! He won't have a dollar when he goes home tonight."

As if to verify Kinkaid's prophecy, Llewellyn made a large wager and lost. As he consulted his book for the next number, the boy came up again and placed a glass of clear water beside him. Llewellyn emptied his whisky glass at one gulp and immediately drank the water. Shoving the two empty glasses to one side, he made his next play.

Again he lost. He doubled on the following spin; and lost again. Then he redoubled, and once more he lost. He was playing Black 20 and Red 5, and on the next turn he halved his former bet between Red 21 and Black 4. "Eleven" came. He now quartered, playing 17, 18, 20 and 21 with one stack, and 4, 5, 7 and 8 with another. "Eleven" repeated.

When Bloodgood had raked in the chips Llewellyn

sat staring at the green cloth without moving. For fully five minutes he remained thus, letting the plays pass without paying any attention. Once or twice he brushed his hand across his eyes and shook his head violently, as if some confusion of mind were overpowering him.

Vance had moved forward a step and was watching him intently, and Kinkaid, too, appeared deeply concerned about Llewellyn's behavior. Bloodgood glanced at him from time to time, but without any indication of more than a casual interest.

Llewellyn's face had now turned scarlet, and he pressed the palms of his hands to his temples and breathed deeply, as a man will do when his head throbs with pain and he experiences a sense of suffocation.

Suddenly, as though he were making a great effort, he sprang to his feet, upsetting his chair, and turned from the table. His hands had fallen to his sides. He took three or four steps, staggered, and then collapsed in a distorted heap on the floor.

A slight commotion followed, and several of the men on Llewellyn's side of the table crowded about the prostrate figure. But two of the uniformed attendants at the entrance hurried forward, and, elbowing their way through the spectators, lifted Llewellyn and carried him toward Kinkaid's private office. Kinkaid was already at the door, holding it open for them when they reached it with the motion-less form.

Vance and I followed them into the office before Kinkaid had time to close the door.

"What do you want here?" snapped Kinkaid.

"I'm stayin' a while," Vance returned in a cold, firm voice. "Put it down to youthful curiosity—if you must have a reason."

Kinkaid snorted and waved the two attendants out.

"Here, Van," requested Vance; "help me lift the chap into that straight chair."

We raised Llewellyn into the chair, and Vance held the man's body far forward so that his head hung between his knees. I noticed that Llewellyn's face had lost all its color and was now a deathly white. Vance felt for his pulse and then turned to Kinkaid, who stood rigidly by the desk, a faint cynical sneer on his mouth.

"Any smelling salts?" Vance asked.

Kinkaid drew out one of the desk drawers and handed Vance a squat green bottle which Vance took and held under Llewellyn's nose.

At this moment Bloodgood opened the office door, stepped inside, and closed it quickly behind him.

"What's the trouble?" he asked Kinkaid. There was a look of alarm on his face.

"Get back to the table," Kinkaid ordered angrily. "There's no trouble. . . . Can't a man faint?"

Bloodgood hesitated, shot a searching look at Vance, shrugged his shoulders, and went out.

Vance again tried Llewellyn's pulse, forced the man's head back, and, lifting one of the eyelids, inspected the eye. Then he placed Llewellyn on the floor and slipped a flat leather cushion, from one of the chairs, under his head.

"He hasn't fainted, Kinkaid," Vance said, rising and facing the other grimly. "He's been poisoned. . . ."

"Rot!" The word was a guttural ejaculation.

"Do you know a doctor in the neighborhood?" Vance's tone was significantly calm.

Kinkaid drew in his breath audibly.

"There's one next door. But——"

"Get him!" commanded Vance. "And be quick about it."

Kinkaid stood in rigid resentment for a brief moment; then he turned to the telephone on the desk and dialed a number. After a pause he cleared his throat and spoke in a strained voice.

"Doctor Rogers? . . . This is Kinkaid. There's been an accident here. Come right away. . . . Thanks."

He banged the receiver down and turned to Vance with a muttered oath.

"A sweet mess!" he complained furiously.

He stepped to a small stand beside the desk, on

which stood a silver water-service, and, picking up
the carafe, inverted it over one of the crystal glasses.
The carafe was empty.

"Hell!" he grumbled. He pressed a button in one
of the walnut panels of the east wall. "I'm going to
have a brandy. How about you?" He gave Vance a
sour look.

"Thanks awfully," murmured Vance.

The door leading into the bar opened and an attendant appeared.

"*Courvoisier,*" Kinkaid ordered. "And fill that
bottle," he added, pointing to the water-service.

The man picked up the carafe and returned to the
bar. (He had started slightly at the sight of Llewellyn's body on the floor, but by no other sign had he
indicated that there was anything amiss. Kinkaid
had chosen his personnel with shrewd discrimination.)

When the cognac had been brought in and served,
Kinkaid drank his in one swallow. Vance was still
sipping his when one of the uniformed men from
the reception hall below rapped on the door and
admitted the doctor, a large rotund man with a
benevolent, almost childlike, face.

"There's your patient," Kinkaid rasped, jerking
his thumb toward Llewellyn. "What's the verdict?"

Doctor Rogers knelt down beside the prone figure,
mumbling as he did so: "Lucky you caught me.
. . . Had a confinement—just got in. . . ."

He made a rapid examination: he looked at Llewellyn's pupils, took his pulse, put the stethoscope to his heart, and felt his wrists and the back of his neck. As he worked he asked several questions regarding what had preceded Llewellyn's present condition. It was Vance who answered all of the questions, describing Llewellyn's nervousness at the roulette table, his high color, and his sudden prostration.

"Looks like a case of poisoning," Doctor Rogers told Kinkaid, opening his medicine case swiftly and preparing a hypodermic injection. "I can't say what it is yet. He's in a stupor. Small, accelerated pulse; rapid, shallow respiration; dilated pupils . . . all symptoms of acute toxæmia. What you tell me of the flush, the staggering and the collapse; and now the pallor—all point to some sort of poison. . . . I'm giving him a hypo of caffein. It's all I can do here. . . ." He rose ponderously and threw the syringe back into his bag. "Must get him to a hospital immediately—he needs heroic treatment. I'll call an ambulance. . . ." And he waddled to the telephone.

Kinkaid stepped forward: he was again the cool, poker-faced gambler.

"Get him to the nearest hospital—the best you know," he said, in a businesslike voice. "I'll take care of everything."

Doctor Rogers nodded.

"The Park End—it's in the neighborhood." And he began dialing a number clumsily.

Vance moved toward the door.

"I think I'll be staggerin' along," he drawled. His face was grim, and he gave Kinkaid a long significant look. "Interestin' letter I received—eh, what? . . . Cheerio!"

A few minutes later we were out in 73rd Street. It was a raw cold night, and a chilling drizzle had begun to fall.

Vance's car was parked a hundred feet or so west of the entrance to the Casino, and as we walked toward it, Detectives Snitkin and Hennessey * stepped out of the doorway of a near-by house.

"Everything all right, Mr. Vance?" Snitkin asked, in a low, sepulchral voice.

"'Pon my word!" exclaimed Vance. "What are you two gallant sleuths doing here on a night like this?"

"Sergeant Heath† told us to come up here and hang around the Casino, in case you might want us," Snitkin explained. "The Sergeant said you were expecting something to break around here."

"Really! Did he, now? Fancy that!" Vance appeared puzzled. "Stout fella, the Sergeant. . . .

* Snitkin and Hennessey were two of the members of the Homicide Bureau who had participated in several of Vance's famous criminal cases.

† Sergeant Ernest Heath, of the Homicide Bureau, had been officially in charge of all the cases which Vance had investigated.

However, everything is taken care of. I'm dashed grateful to you for coming, but there's no earthly reason for you to hover about any longer. I'm toddlin' off to bed myself."

But instead of going home he drove to Markham's apartment in West 11th Street.

Markham, much to my surprise, was still up, and greeted us cordially in his drawing-room.* When we had settled ourselves before the gas-logs Vance turned to him with a questioning air.

"Snitkin and Hennessey were guarding me like good fellows tonight," he said. "Do you, by any chance, ken the reason for such solicitous devotion?"

Markham smiled, a bit shamefacedly.

"The truth is, Vance," he apologetically explained; "after I left your apartment this afternoon I got to thinking there might be something in that letter, after all; and I called up Sergeant Heath and told him—as near as I could remember—everything that was in it. I also told him you had decided to go to the Casino tonight to watch young Llewellyn. I suppose he thought it might be just as well to send a couple of the boys up there to be on hand in case there *was* any truth in the letter."

"That explains it," nodded Vance. "There was no

* The same room, it flashed through my mind, in which the momentous and dramatic poker game was played in the "Canary" murder case.

need, however, for the bodyguard. But the letter proved amazingly prophetic."

"What's that!" Markham swung round in his chair.

"Yes, yes. Quite a prognosticatin' epistle." Vance took a deep draw on his cigarette. "Lynn Llewellyn was poisoned before my eyes."

Markham sprang to his feet and stared at Vance. "Dead?"

"He wasn't when I left him. But I didn't tarry." Vance was thoughtful. "He was in bad shape though. He's under the care of a Doctor Rogers at the Park End Hospital. . . . Deuced curious situation. I'm rather confused." He, too, got up. "Wait a bit." He went into the den, and I heard him at the telephone.

In a few minutes he returned.

"I've just talked to the pudgy Æsculapius at the hospital," he reported. "Llewellyn's about the same— except that his respiration has become slower and more shallow. His pressure is down to seventy over fifty, and he's having convulsive movements. . . . Everything's being done that's possible—adrenalin, caffein, digitalis, and gastric lavage by the nasal route. No positive diagnosis possible, of course. Very mystifyin', Markham. . . "

Just then the telephone rang and Markham

answered it. A minute later he emerged from the den. His face was pale, and there were deep corrugations on his forehead. He came back to the centre-table, like a man in a daze.

"Good God, Vance!" he muttered. "Something devilish *is* going on. That was Heath on the wire. A call has just come through to Headquarters. Heath relayed it to me—because of that letter, I imagine. . . ."

Markham paused, looking out into space; and Vance glanced up at him curiously.

"And what, pray, was the burden of the Sergeant's song?"

Markham, as if with considerable effort, turned his eyes back to Vance.

"Llewellyn's young wife is dead—poisoned!"

CHAPTER IV

THE DEAD GIRL'S ROOM

(Sunday, October 16; 1:30 a. m.)

Vance's eyebrows went up sharply.

"My word! I didn't expect that." He took his cigarette from his mouth and looked at it with concern. "And yet . . . there may be a pattern. I say, Markham, did the Sergeant happen to say what time the lady died?"

"No." Markham shook his head abstractedly. "A doctor was summoned first, it seems; and then the call was sent through to Headquarters. We can assume that death occurred about half an hour ago——"

"Half an hour!" Vance tapped the arm of his chair in thoughtful tattoo. "Just about the time Llewellyn collapsed. . . . Simultaneity, what? . . Queer—deuced queer. . . . No other information?"

"No, nothing more. Heath was just hopping a car with some of the boys, headed for the Llewellyn house. He'll probably phone again when he gets there."

Vance threw his cigarette on the hearth and rose.

"We sha'n't be here, however," he said, with a curiously grim intonation, turning toward Markham. "We're going to Park Avenue to find out for ourselves. I don't like this thing, Markham—I don't at all like it. There's something fiendish and sinister—and abnormal—going on. I felt it when I first read that letter. Some terrible killer is abroad, and these two poisonings may be only the beginning. A poisoner is the worst of all criminals,—there's no knowing how far he may go. . . . Come."

I had rarely seen Vance so perturbed and insistent; and Markham, feeling the force of his resolution and his fears, permitted himself, without protest, to be driven in Vance's car to the old Llewellyn mansion on Park Avenue.

The house, of brownstone, stood back a few yards from the Avenue. A high black scroll-iron fence, with a wide iron gate, extended the entire width of the lot, which was about fifty feet; and the shallow areaway had not been paved, but was still set with an old square box hedge, two trimmed cypress trees, and two small rectangular flowerbeds, one on each side of the flagstone walk that led to the massive oak front door.

When we arrived at the Llewellyn home, the police were already there. Two uniformed officers from the local precinct station stood in the areaway. On recognizing the District Attorney, they saluted and came forward.

"Sergeant Heath and some of the boys of the Homicide Squad just went in, Chief," one of them told Markham, thrusting his thumb against the push-button of the door-bell.

The front door was immediately opened by a tall, thin, and very pale man in a black-and-white checked dressing-gown.

"I'm the District Attorney," Markham told him, "and I want to see Sergeant Heath. He came a few minutes ago, I believe."

The man bowed with stiff, exaggerated dignity.

"Certainly, sir," he said, with an oily, slightly cockney accent. "Won't you come in, sir. . . . The police officers are upstairs—in Mrs. Lynn Lewellyn's room at the south end of the hall.—I'm the butler, sir, and I was told to remain here at the door." (This last remark was his apology for not showing us the way.)

We brushed past him and ascended the wide circular stairs, which were brilliantly lighted. As we reached the first landing, Detective Sullivan, standing in the hall above, greeted Markham.

"Howdy, Chief. The Sergeant'll be glad you've come. It looks like a dirty job." And he led the way down the hall.

In the south wing of the house Sullivan threw

open a door for us. We entered a room which was
large and almost square, with a high ceiling, an old-
fashioned carved mantelpiece, and heavy over-drapes
of a bygone era hanging from the great double-
shuttered windows. The furniture—all Empire—
looked authentic and costly; and hanging on the
walls were many rare old prints which would have
been an asset to any art museum.

On the high canopied bed to our left lay the still
figure of a woman of about thirty. The silk cover
had been partly thrown back, and both her arms
were drawn up over her head. Her hair was brushed
back flat, and over it was a hair-net, tied at the back
of her neck.

Her face, under a layer of recently applied cold-
cream, was cyanosed and blotchy, as if she had died
in a convulsion; and her eyes were wide open and
staring. It was an unlovely and blood-chilling sight.

Sergeant Heath, two members of the Homicide
Bureau—Detectives Burke and Guilfoyle—and a
Lieutenant Smalley, from the local station, were in
the room. The Sergeant was seated at the large
marble-topped centre-table, his note-book before him.

Facing the table stood a tall vigorous woman of
about sixty, with a strong aquiline face. She was
dabbing her eyes with a small lace handkerchief.
Though I had never seen her before, I recognized
her, from pictures that had appeared in the

newspapers from time to time, as Mrs. Anthony Llewellyn.

Near her stood a young woman who looked singularly like Lynn Llewellyn, and I rightly assumed that she was Amelia Llewellyn, Lynn's sister. Her dark hair was parted in the middle and combed straight back over her ears to a twisted knot low on the back of her head. Her face, like her mother's, was strong and aquiline, with a marked hardness and an almost contemptuous expression. She glanced at us, when we entered, with a cold and indifferent, and somewhat bored, look. Both women were wearing silk tufted dressing-gowns, cut on the lines of a Japanese kimono.

Before the mantel stood a slender, nervous man of about thirty-five, in dinner clothes, smoking a cigarette in a long ivory holder. We soon learned that he was Doctor Allan Kane, a friend of Miss Llewellyn's, who lived within a block of the Llewellyn home, and who had been called in by Miss Llewellyn. It was Doctor Kane who had informed the police of young Mrs. Llewellyn's death. Kane, though he appeared to be agitated, had an air of professional seriousness. His face was flushed, and he kept shifting his weight from one foot to the other; but his gaze was direct and appraising as he looked at each of us in turn.

Sergeant Heath rose and greeted us as we came in. "I was hoping you'd come, Mr. Markham," he said, with an air of obvious relief. "But I wasn't expecting Mr. Vance. I thought he'd be at the Casino."

"I was at the Casino, Sergeant," Vance told him in a serious low tone. "And thanks awfully for Snitkin and Hennessey. But I didn't need them. . . ."

"Lynn!" The name, like an agonized wail, split the gloomy atmosphere of the room. It had come from the lips of Mrs. Llewellyn; and she turned to Vance with a face distorted with apprehension. "Did you see my son there? And is he all right?"

Vance regarded the woman for several moments, as if making up his mind how to answer her question. Then he said sympathetically but with determined precision:

"I regret, madam, that your son, too, has been poisoned——"

"My son dead?" The intensity of her words sent a chill through me.

Vance shook his head, his eyes fixed intently on the distracted woman.

"Not at the last report. He's under a doctor's care at the Park End Hospital——"

"I must go to him!" she cried, starting from the room.

But Vance restrained her gently.

"No; not just now, please," he said in a firm kindly voice. "You could do no good. And you are needed here at present. I will get a report from the hospital for you in a little while. . . . I regret having had to bring you this sad news, madam; but you would have had to hear it sooner or later. . . . Please sit down and help us."

The woman drew herself up and squared her jaw with Spartan fortitude.

"It can never be said that we Llewellyns ever shirked our duty," she announced, in a hard stern voice; and she sat down rigidly in a chair at the foot of the bed.

Amelia Llewellyn had been watching her mother with cynical indifference.

"That's all very noble," she commented, with a shrug. " 'We Llewellyns'—the usual abracadabra. *'Firmitas et fortitudo,'* the family motto. A gryphon *rampant* or *sejant* or *couchant*—I forget which. In any event, a gryphon is a chimerical creature. Quite characteristic of our family: capable of anything— and nothing."

"Perhaps the Llewellyn gryphon is *segreant,*" Vance suggested, looking straight at the girl.

She caught her breath, stared back at Vance for a few seconds, and then replied cynically: "It might be, at that. The Llewellyns are rather flighty."

Vance continued to regard her closely, and after a moment she walked up to him with a twisted smile.

"So, darling little Lynn—the filial paragon—has

also been poisoned?" she said; and the smile faded from her mouth. "Some one is evidently determined to make a nice thorough job of it. I wouldn't be surprised if I were next. . . . There's too much rotten money in this family."

She shot a sneering look at her mother, who glared at her angrily; and then, sitting down on the edge of the table, she lighted a cigarette.

Markham was impatient and annoyed.

"Get on with your work, Sergeant," he ordered brusquely. "Who found this young woman?" He waved his hand distastefully toward the bed.

"I did." Amelia Llewellyn became serious, and her breast rose and fell with emotion.

"Ah!" Vance sat down and studied the girl quizzically. "Suppose you tell us the circumstances, Miss Llewellyn."

"We all went to bed round eleven," she began. "Uncle Dick and Mr. Bloodgood had gone to the Casino right after dinner. Lynn followed about an hour later. And Allan—Doctor Kane here—had some calls to make, and left with Lynn. . . ."

"Just a moment," broke in Vance, holding up his hand. "I understood the dinner tonight was more or less a family affair. Was Doctor Kane present?"

"Yes, he was here." The girl nodded bitterly. "I knew what another of these anniversary affairs would be—bickerings, recriminations, general squabbling.

And I was nervous. So, at the last minute, I asked Doctor Kane to come to dinner. I thought his presence might tone down the animosity. Of course, Morgan Bloodgood was here too, but he's really like one of the family: we never hesitate to air our differences in his presence."

"And did Doctor Kane wield a restraining influence on the gathering tonight?" asked Vance.

"I'm afraid not," she returned. "There was too much pent-up passion that had to have an outlet."

Vance hesitated and then went on with his questioning:

"So Lynn and your uncle and the others departed; and you and your sister-in-law and your mother retired about eleven. Then what happened?"

"I was upset and fidgety and couldn't sleep. I got up around midnight and started to sketch. I worked for an hour or so, and had just decided to turn in when I heard Virginia cry out in a hysterical voice. My room is in this wing of the house; and the two apartments are divided only by a short private passageway which I use as a clothes closet." She indicated, with a movement of her head, a door at the rear of the room.

"You could hear your sister-in-law call out with the two doors and the passageway between you?" Vance asked.

"Ordinarily, I couldn't have heard her," the girl

explained; "but I had just gone into the clothes closet to hang up my dressing-gown."

"And what did you do then?"

"I stepped to the door there to listen, and Virginia sounded as if she were choking. I tried the door and found it unlocked. . . ."

"Was it unusual for this door to be unlocked?" Vance interrupted.

"No. In fact, it is seldom locked."

"Continue, please."

"Well," the girl went on, "Virginia was lying on the bed, as she is now. Her eyes were staring; her face was terribly red; and she was in a horrible convulsion. I ran out into the hall and called to mother. Mother came in and looked at her. 'Get a doctor, Amelia,' she said; and I immediately phoned to Doctor Kane. He lives only a short distance from here, and he came right over. Before I was through phoning, Virginia seemed to collapse. She became very still—too still. I—I knew that she had died. . . ." The girl shuddered involuntarily, and her voice trailed off.

"And now, Doctor Kane?" Vance turned toward the man standing by the mantel.

Kane came forward nervously: his hand trembled as he took his cigarette holder from his lips.

"When I arrived, sir, a few minutes later," he began, with a studied air of professional dignity,

"Mrs. Llewellyn—Mrs. Lynn Llewellyn, I mean, of course—was quite dead. Her eyes were staring; her pupils were so widely dilated that I could hardly see the retina; and she was covered with a scarlatiniform rash. She seemed to have a *post-mortem* rise of temperature, and the position of her arms and the distortion of her facial and neck muscles indicated that she had had a convulsion and died of asphyxia. It looked like some poison in the belladonna group— hyoscin, atropin, or scopolamin. I did not move the body, and I warned both Mrs. Llewellyn and her daughter not to touch her. I immediately telephoned to the police."

"Quite correct," murmured Vance. "And then you waited for our arrival?"

"Naturally." Kane had regained much of his self-control, though his face was still flushed and he breathed heavily.

"And nothing in the room has been touched?"

"Nothing. I have been here all the time, and Miss Llewellyn and her mother waited here with me."

Vance nodded slowly.

"By the by, doctor," he asked, "do you use a type-writer?"

Kane gave a slight start of surprise.

"Why—yes," he stammered. "I used to type my papers at medical school. I'm not very good at it, though. I—I don't understand. . . . But if my typing can be of any help in the matter——"

"Merely an idle question," Vance returned casually, and then turned to Heath. "The Medical Examiner been notified?"

"Sure." The Sergeant was sullen and chewed viciously on his black cigar. "The call went through to the office in the usual way, but I phoned Doremus * at his home,—I didn't like the set-up tonight. . . ."

"And he was probably much annoyed," suggested Vance.

The Sergeant grunted.

"I'll say he was. But I told him Mr. Markham might be here, and he said he'd come himself. He oughta be here pretty soon."

Vance rose and faced Kane.

"I think that will be all for the present, doctor. But I must ask you to remain until the Medical Examiner comes. You may be able to assist him. . . . Would you mind waiting in the drawing-room downstairs?"

"Certainly not." He bowed stiffly and went toward the door. "I'll be glad to help in any way I can."

When he had gone Vance turned to the two women.

"I'm sorry to have to ask you to remain up," he said, "but I'm afraid it's necess'ry Will you be so good as to wait in your rooms." His voice, though

* Doctor Emanuel Doremus, the Chief Medical Examiner of New York.

mild and gracious, held an undertone of command.

Mrs. Llewellyn stood up and her eyes blazed.

"Why can't I go to my son?" she demanded. "There's nothing more I can do here. I know nothing at all about this affair."

"You cannot help your son," Vance replied firmly; "and you may be able to help us. I'll be glad, however, to get the hospital's report for you."

He went to the telephone on the night-stand; and a minute later he was talking with Doctor Rogers. When he had replaced the receiver he turned to Mrs. Llewellyn encouragingly.

"Your son has come out of his coma, madam," he reported. "And he is breathing more normally; his pulse is stronger; and he seems to be out of danger. You will be notified immediately if there should be any change for the worse."

Mrs. Llewellyn, holding her handkerchief close to her face, went out sobbing.

Amelia Llewellyn did not go at once. She waited till the door had closed behind her mother, and then looked at Vance questioningly.

"Why," she asked in a dead, metallic voice, "did you ask Doctor Kane if he used a typewriter?"

Vance took out the letter that had brought him into the affair, and handed it to her without a word. He watched her closely with half-closed eyes as she read it. A troubled frown settled over her face, but

she showed no surprise. When she had come to the
end she slowly and deliberately refolded the letter
and handed it back to Vance.

"Thanks," she said, and turning, started toward
the door to the passageway leading to her quarters.

"One moment, Miss Llewellyn." Vance's summon-
ing voice halted her just as she placed her hand on
the knob; and she faced the room again. "Do you,
too, use a typewriter?"

The girl nodded lethargically.

"Oh, yes. I do all of my correspondence on a small
typewriter I have. . . . However," she added, with
a faint, weary smile, "I'm much more adept than the
person who typed that letter."

"And are the other members of the household given
to using the typewriter, too?" asked Vance.

"Yes—we're all quite modern." The girl spoke
indifferently. "Even mother types her own lectures.
And Uncle Dick, having been an author at one time,
developed a rapid, but sloppy, two-fingered system."

"And your sister-in-law: did she use one?"

The girl's eyes turned toward the bed, and she
winced.

"Yes. Virginia played around with the machine
when Lynn was out gambling. . . . Lynn himself is
quite proficient as a typist. He once attended a commercial school—probably thought he might be called
on some time to handle the Llewellyn estate. But

mother wasn't thinking along those lines; so he turned to night-clubs instead." (There was a curious detachment in her manner which I could not fathom at the time.)

"That leaves only Mr. Bloodgood——" Vance began; but the girl quickly interrupted him.

"He types, also." Her eyes darkened somewhat, and I felt that her attitude toward Bloodgood was not altogether a friendly one. "He typed most of his reports of that slot-machine affair he was connected with on our typewriter downstairs."

Vance raised his eyebrows slightly in mild interest.

"There is a typewriter downstairs?"

Again the girl nodded, and shrugged as if the matter was of no interest to her.

"There always has been one there—in the little library off the drawing-room."

"Do you think," asked Vance, "that the letter I showed you was typed on that machine?"

"It might have been." The girl sighed. "It's the same kind of type and the same color ribbon. . . . But there are so many like it."

"And perhaps," Vance pursued, "you could suggest who is the author of the communication."

Amelia Llewellyn's face clouded, and the hard look returned to her eyes.

"I could make several suggestions," she said in

a dull angry tone. "But I have no intention of doing anything of the kind." And opening the door with decisive swiftness, she went from the room.

"You learned a hell of a lot!" snorted Heath with ponderous sarcasm. "This house is just a bunch of stenographers."

Vance regarded the Sergeant indulgently.

"I learned a good deal, don't y' know."

Heath shifted the cigar between his teeth and made a grimace.

"Maybe yes and maybe no," he rumbled. "The case is cock-eyed anyway, if you ask me.—Llewellyn getting poisoned at the Casino, and his wife having it handed to her here at the same time. Looks to me as if there was a gang at work."

"The same person could have accomplished both acts, Sergeant," Vance returned mildly. "In fact, I feel sure it was the same person. Furthermore, I think it was that person who sent me the letter. . . . Just a minute."

He walked to the night-stand, and, moving the telephone aside, picked up a small folded piece of paper.

"I saw this when I called the hospital," he explained. "But I purposely didn't look at it till the ladies should have left us."

He unfolded the paper and held it under the night-light on the table. From where I stood I could see that it was a single sheet of pale-blue note-paper, and that there was typing on it.

"Oh, my aunt!" Vance murmured, as he read it. "Amazin'! . . . "

At length he handed the paper to Markham, who held it so that Heath and I, who were standing at his side, could see it. It was an inexpertly typed note, and ran:

> Dear Lynn—I cannot make you happy, and God knows, no one in this house has ever tried to make *me* happy. Uncle Dick is the only person here who has ever been civil or considerate toward me. I am not wanted here and am utterly miserable. I am going to poison myself.
>
> Good-by—and may your new roulette system bring you the fortune that you seem to want more than you want anything else.

The signature, "Virginia," was also typewritten. Markham folded the note and pursed his lips. He looked at Vance for a long time; then he remarked:

"That seems to simplify matters."

"Oh, my dear fellow!" Vance protested. "That note merely complicates the situation abominably."

CHAPTER V

POISON!

(Sunday, October 16; 2:15 a. m.)

At that moment Sullivan opened the door and admitted Doctor Doremus, a slight jaunty person with a businesslike, peppery air. He wore a tweed top-coat, and the brim of his pearl-gray felt hat was turned down rakishly on one side.

He greeted us with dramatic consternation, and then cocked an eye flippantly at Sergeant Heath.

"When you don't call me to see your corpses at meal time," he complained with falsetto ill-nature, "you wait till I'm sound asleep and then rout me out. No system . . . no system. It's a conspiracy to rob me of food and rest. I've aged twenty years since I took this job three years ago."

"You look young and snappy enough," grinned Heath. (He had long since become accustomed to the Medical Examiner's grousing.)

"Well, it's through no kindly consideration on the part of you babies in the Homicide Bureau, by Gad!" Doremus snapped. "Where's the body?" His eyes shot round the room and came to rest on the still figure of Virginia Llewellyn. "A lady, eh? What did she die of?"

"*You* tell us." Heath had suddenly become aggressive.

Doremus grunted; then, removing his hat and coat, he put them on a chair and approached the bed. For ten minutes he was examining the dead girl, and, once again, I was impressed by his competency and thoroughness. For all his nonchalant mannerisms and cynical attitude, he was a shrewd and efficient physician—one of the best and most conscientious medical examiners New York has ever had.

While Doremus was busy with his gruesome task Vance made a brief inspection of the room. He went first to the night-table on which stood a small silver water-service similar to the one in Kinkaid's office at the Casino. He picked up the two glasses and looked at them: they both seemed to be dry. He then took the stopper from the carafe, and inverted the bottle over one of the glasses. It was empty. Vance frowned as he set it back on the tray. After inspecting the interior of the little drawer in the table, he walked toward the bathroom door, which was half open, at the rear of the room.

As he passed Markham he commented in a low voice:

"The general service tonight has been abominable.

Kinkaid's water carafe was empty; and so is the Lynn Llewellyns'. Queer, don't y' know. . . . Incidentally, the drawer in that table by the bed contains only a handkerchief, a pack of cards—for solitaire, no doubt,—a pencil and pad, a stick of lip pomade, and a pair of reading glasses. . . . Nothing lethal, as it were."

I followed Vance into the bathroom, for I knew that he had something definite in mind when he began his tour of inspection:—this fact was clearly indicated by his casual and lazy manner, which he invariably assumed in moments of highest tension.

The bathroom was quite a large one, thoroughly modernized, and had two small windows facing on the south court. The room was neatly arranged and everything was in order. Vance, after switching on the light, glanced about him searchingly. There was a small atomizer and a tube of bath tablets on one of the window sills.

Vance pressed the bulb of the atomizer and sniffed at the spray.

"Derline's *Fleur-de-lis*, Van," he remarked. "Ideal for blondes." He read the label on the tube of bath tablets. "Also Derline's *Fleur-de-lis*. Quite consistent and correct. Alas, too many women make the fatal error of contrasting their bath perfume with their personal scent. . . ."

He opened the door of the medicine cabinet and

looked inside. It contained only the usual items: cleansing creams and skin food, a bottle of hand lotion, toilet water, talcum and bath powders, a deodorant, a tube of tooth paste, dental floss, a thermometer, and the conventional array of medicinal preparations—iodin, aspirin, sodium bicarbonate, camphor, Dobell's solution, yellow throat mixture, glycerin, argyrol, aromatic spirits of ammonia, benzoin, milk of magnesia, bromide tablets, a standard eye-wash with its cup-shaped stopper, medicated alcohol, and so forth.

Vance spent considerable time scrutinizing each item. At length he took down a small brown bottle with a printed label, and, carefully adjusting his monocle, read the fine type of the formula. Then he slipped the bottle into his pocket, closed the cabinet door, and turned back into the bedroom.

Doctor Doremus was just putting the sheet back over the still form on the bed. He turned toward Heath with simulated truculence.

"Well, what about it?" he demanded irritably, spreading his hands in a gesture of inquiry. "She's dead—if that's what you want to know. And I have to be dragged out of the blankets at two in the morning to tell you that!"

Heath took his cigar slowly from between his teeth and glowered at the Medical Examiner.

"All right, doc," he said. "She's dead, says you.

But how long has she been that way, and what killed her?"

"I knew that was coming," sighed Doremus, and then became professionally serious. "Well, Sergeant, she's been dead about two hours; and she was poisoned. . . . Now, I suppose you'll want me to tell you where she got the poison." And he leered at Heath.

Vance stepped between the two men.

"A doctor who was called in," he said gravely to Doremus, "suggested that she might have died from one of the poisons in the belladonna group."

"Any third-year medical student would know that," Doremus returned. "Sure, it's belladonna poisoning. . . . Was this saw-bones here in time to catch her *post-mortem* rise in temperature?"

Vance nodded.

"He was here within ten minutes of her death."

"Well, there you are." Doremus put on his coat and carefully adjusted his hat on the side of his head. "All the indications: staring eyes, widely dilated pupils, pin-point rash, a jump in temperature, signs of convulsions and asphyxia. . . . Simple."

"Yes, yes—quite." Vance drew forth the bottle he had taken from the bathroom cabinet, and handed it to the Medical Examiner. "Could these tablets have been the cause of death?" he asked.

Doremus looked closely at the label and the printed formula.

"Regulation rhinitis tablets—household-remedy stuff." He held the bottle under the table light and squinted at it. "Powdered camphor," he read aloud; "fluid extract of belladonna root, a quarter minim; and quinin sulphate. . . . Certainly this could have done it—if enough of 'em were taken."

"The bottle's empty; and it contained a hundred tablets originally," Vance pointed out.

Doctor Doremus, still scrutinizing the label, nodded his head.

"A hundred times one-quarter of a minim would be twenty-five minims. . . . Enough belladonna to knock anybody cold." He handed the bottle back to Vance. "That's the answer. Why get me up in the middle of the night when you had all the dope?"

"Really, doctor," returned Vance quietly, "we're merely probin' around. I just found this empty bottle, d' ye see, and thought I'd advance it as a possibility."

"Looks all right to me." Doremus went to the door. "Only a *post mortem*'ll answer your questions definitely."

Markham spoke up brusquely.

"That's just what we want, doctor. When is the soonest we can have the autopsy report?"

"Oh, Lord!" Doremus set his teeth. "And to-

morrow's Sunday. This modern speed will kill me
yet. . . . How would eleven o'clock tomorrow
morning do?"

"That would be eminently satisfactory," Markham
told him.

Doctor Doremus took a small pad from his pocket,
and, writing something on it, tore off the top sheet
and handed it to the Sergeant.

"Here's your order for the removal of the body."

The Sergeant pocketed the slip of paper.

"The body'll be at the morgue before you are," he
mumbled.

"That's bully." Doremus gave Heath a vicious
leer and opened the door. "And now I'm going back
to sleep. You can have a massacre tonight if you
want to, but you won't see me again till nine a. m."
He waved his hand in a farewell gesture which
included us all, and went swiftly out.

When the Medical Examiner had slammed the door
behind him, Markham turned to Vance gravely.

"Where'd you find that bottle, Vance?"

"In yon *lavatorium*. It was the only thing I saw
there that seemed to have any possibilities."

"Taken in connection with that suicide note
you found," observed Markham, "it would seem
to furnish a simple explanation of this terrible
affair."

Vance regarded Markham thoughtfully for several

moments; then, after a long inhalation on his cigarette, he walked the length of the room and back, his head bowed in contemplation.

"I'm not so sure, Markham," he murmured, almost as if to himself. "I'll grant you that it's a specious solution of the death of this girl on the bed. But what of that poor johnnie in the hospital? It wasn't belladonna that hit him; and there certainly wasn't any suicidal urge in *his* mind. He was playing to win tonight; and his silly system was apparently working out. Yet, in the midst of it he fades out. . . . No, no. The empty bottle of rhinitis tablets is too simple. And this affair is not simple at all. It's filled with shadows and false scents: it has hidden subtleties and convolutions. . . ."

"After all, you found the bottle——" began Markham. But Vance interrupted him.

"That may have been arranged for us. It fits too snugly into the pattern. We'll know more—or less— tomorrow morning when Doremus has turned in his report."

Markham was annoyed.

"Why try to concoct mysteries?"

"My dear Markham!" Vance reproached him, and stood for several minutes apparently absorbed in one of the eighteenth-century prints hanging over the mantel.

Heath, in the meantime, had been telephoning to

the Department of Public Welfare for a wagon to take the body away. When he had completed the call he spoke to Lieutenant Smalley of the local precinct station, who had watched the proceedings silently from a corner of the room.

"There's nothing more, Lieutenant. Mr. Markham's here, and there's only routine stuff till Doc Doremus makes the autopsy. But you might leave a couple of your men on the job outside."

"Anything you want, Sergeant." Lieutenant Smalley shook hands all round, and went out with an air of obvious relief.

"I think we can go, too," Markham said. "You're in charge, of course, Sergeant—I'll arrange it with the Inspector the first thing in the morning."

"I say, Markham," Vance put in, "let's not dash precipitately away. I could bear to know a few facts, and as long as we're here tonight. . . ."

"What, for instance, do you want to know?" Markham was impatient.

Vance turned away from the print, and gazed sadly at the dead girl.

"I'd like a few more words with Doctor Kane before we drift out into the chillin' mist."

Markham made a wry face, but finally nodded in reluctant assent.

"He's downstairs." And he led the way out into the hall.

Doctor Kane was pacing nervously up and down when we entered the drawing-room.

"What's the report?" he asked before Vance had time to speak.

"The Medical Examiner merely corroborated your own diagnosis, doctor," Vance told him. "The *post mortem* will be performed the first thing in the morning. . . . By the by, doctor, are you the Llewellyns' family physician?"

"I can hardly say that," the other answered. "I doubt if they have any one attend them regularly. They don't require much medical supervision; they're a very healthy family. I do prescribe occasionally, though, for minor ailments—but as a friend rather than professionally."

"And have you done any prescribing for any of them lately?" asked Vance.

Kane took a moment to think.

"Nothing of any consequence," he answered at length. "I suggested a tonic of iron—Blaud's Mass —and strychnin for Miss Llewellyn a few days ago——"

"Has Lynn Llewellyn any constitutional ailment," interrupted Vance, "that would cause him to collapse under keen excitement?"

"No-o. He has a hypertrophied heart, with the attendant increased blood-pressure—the result of athletics in college——"

"Angina?"

Kane shook his head.

"Nothing as serious as that—though his condition may develop into that some day."

"Ever prescribe for him?"

"A year or so ago I gave him a prescription for some nitroglycerin tablets—a two-hundredth of a grain. But that's all."

"Nitroglycerin—eh, what?" A flash of interest animated Vance's smouldering eyes. "That's most revealin'. . . . And his wife: were you ever called upon in her behalf?"

"Oh, once or twice," Kane answered, with a careless wave of his cigarette holder. "She had rather weak eyes, and I recommended an ordinary eye solution. . . . It's been my experience," he added in a pompous tone, "that very light blondes with pale blue eyes—lack of pigmentation, you understand—have weaker eyes than brunettes——"

"Let's not indulge in ophthalmological theory," Vance cut in, with an ingratiating smile. "It's getting beastly late. . . . What else have you prescribed for young Mrs. Llewellyn?"

"That's really about all." Kane, for all his attempt at poise, was becoming nervous. "I recommended a certain salve for a mild erythema on one of her hands several months ago; and last week, when she had an annoying cold in the head, I suggested regulation rhinitis tablets. I don't recall anything else——"

"Rhinitis tablets?" Vance's penetrating gaze was on the man. "How many did you tell her to take?"

"Oh, the usual dose," Kane returned, with an effort at carelessness, "one or two tablets every two hours."

"Most rhinitis tablets contain belladonna, y' know," remarked Vance in a hard, even tone.

"Why, yes—of course. . . ." Kane's eyes suddenly opened wide, and he stared at Vance with frightened intensity. "But—but, really. . . ." He stammered, and broke off.

"We found an empty hundred-tablet bottle in her medicine cabinet," Vance informed him, without shifting his gaze. "And, according to your own diagnosis, Mrs. Llewellyn died of belladonna poisoning."

Kane's jaw dropped, and his face went pale.

"My God!" he muttered. "She—she couldn't have done that." The man was trembling noticeably. "She would know better—and I was most explicit. . . ."

"No one can blame you in the circumstances, doctor," Vance said consolingly. "Tell me, was Mrs. Llewellyn an intelligent and conscientious patient?"

"Yes—very." Kane moistened his lips with his tongue, and made a valiant effort to control himself. "She was always most careful to follow my instructions implicitly. I remember now that she phoned me, the other day, asking if she could take an extra tablet before the two-hour interval had elapsed."

"And the eye lotion?" asked Vance with marked casualness.

"I'm sure she followed my advice," Kane answered earnestly. "Though, of course, that was an absolutely harmless solution——"

"And what was your advice regarding it?"

"I told her she should bathe her eyes with it every night before retiring."

"What were the ingredients in the unguent you recommended for her hand?"

Kane looked surprised.

"I'm sure I don't know," he returned unsteadily. "The usual simple emollients, I suppose. It was a proprietary preparation, on sale at any drug store, —probably contained zinc oxide or lanolin. There couldn't possibly have been anything harmful in it."

Vance walked to the front window and looked out. He was both puzzled and disturbed.

"Was that the extent of your medical services to Lynn Llewellyn and his wife?" he asked, returning slowly to the centre of the room.

"Yes!" Though Kane's voice quavered, there was in it, nevertheless, a note of undeniable emphasis.

Vance let his eyes rest on the young doctor for a brief period.

"I think that will be all," he said. "There's nothing more you can do here tonight."

Kane drew a deep breath of relief and went to the door.

"Good night, gentlemen," he said, with a questioning look at Vance. "Please call on me if I can be of any help." He opened the door and then hesitated. "I'd be most grateful if you'd let me know the result of the autopsy."

Vance bowed abstractedly.

"We'll be glad to, doctor. And our apologies for having kept you up so late."

Kane did not move for a moment, and I thought he was going to say something; but he suddenly went out, and in a moment we could hear the butler helping him with his coat.

Vance stood at the table for several moments, gazing straight before him and letting his fingers move over the inlaid design of the wood. Then, without shifting his eyes, he sat down and very slowly and deliberately drew out his cigarette-case.

Markham had been standing near the door during this interview, watching both Vance and the doctor intently. He now walked across the room to the marble mantel and leaned against it.

"Vance," he commented gravely, "I'm beginning to see what's in your mind."

Vance looked up and sighed deeply.

"Really, Markham?" He shook his head with a discouraged air. "You're far more penetratin' than I am. I'd give my *ting-yao* vase to know what is in my mind. It's all very confusin'. Everything fits— it's a perfect mosaic. And that's what frightens me."

He shook himself gently, as if to throw off some unpleasant intrusion of thought, and, going to the door, summoned the butler.

"Please tell Miss Llewellyn," he said, when the man appeared, "—I think she is in her own apartment—that we should appreciate her coming to the drawing-room."

When the man had turned down the hall toward the stairs, Vance moved to the mantel and stood beside Markham.

"There are a few other little things I want to know before we make our *adieux*," he explained. He was troubled and restless: I had rarely seen him in such a mood. "No case I have ever helped you with, Markham, has made me feel so strongly the presence of a subtle and devastating personality. Not once has it manifested itself in all the tragic events of this evening; but I know it's there, grinning at us and defying us to penetrate to the bottom of this devilish scheme. And all the ingredients in the plot are, apparently, commonplace and obvious,—but I've a feelin' they're sign-posts pointing *away* from the truth." He smoked a moment in silence; then he said:

"The fiendish part of it is, it's not even intended that we should follow the sign-posts. . . ."

There was the sound of soft footsteps descending the stairs; and a moment later Amelia Llewellyn stood at the drawing-room door.

CHAPTER VI

A CRY IN THE NIGHT

(Sunday, October 16; 3 a. m.)

She had changed her tufted robe for a pair of black satin lounging pyjamas; and I saw evidences of the recent application of rouge, lip-stick and powder. She was smoking a cigarette in an embossed ebony holder; and as she stood before us, framed in the ivory of the door casement, she made a striking figure which somehow reminded me of one of Zuloaga's spectacular poster-paintings.

"I received your verbal subpœna from the jittery yet elegant Crichton—our butler's name is really Smith—and here I am." She spoke with an air of facetious worldliness. "Well, where do we stand now?"

"We much prefer not to stand, Miss Llewellyn," Vance answered, moving a chair forward with a commanding soberness.

"Delighted." She settled herself in the chair and crossed her knees. "I'm frightfully tired, what with all this unusual excitement."

Vance sat down facing her.

"Has it occurred to you, Miss Llewellyn," he asked, "that your brother's wife may have committed suicide?"

"Good Heavens, no!" The girl leaned forward in questioning amazement: she had suddenly dropped her cynical manner.

"You know of no reason, then, why she should have taken her life?" Vance pursued quietly.

"She had no more reason than any one else has." Amelia Llewellyn gazed thoughtfully past Vance. "We could all find some good excuse for suicide. But Virginia had nothing to worry about. She was well provided for, and she was living more comfortably, materially, than she ever had been before." (This remark was made with a decided tinge of bitterness.) "She knew Lynn pretty well before she married him, and she must have calculated every advantage and disadvantage beforehand. Considering the fact that we did not particularly like her, we treated her quite decently—especially mother. But then, Lynn has always been mother's darling, and she'd treat a boa-constrictor with kindness and consideration if Lynn brought it into the house."

"Still," suggested Vance, "even in such circumstances, people do occasionally commit suicide, y' know."

"That's quite true." The girl shrugged. "But Virginia was too cowardly to take her own life, no matter how unhappy she may have been." (A note of animosity informed her voice.) "Besides, she was always self-centred and vain——"

"Vain about what, for instance?" Vance interrupted.

"About everything." She filliped the ashes of her cigarette to the floor. "She was particularly vain about her personal appearance. She was at all times on the stage and in make-up, so to speak."

"Does it not seem possible to you"—Vance was peculiarly persistent—"that if she had been miserable enough——?"

"No!" The girl anticipated the rest of his question with an emphatic denial. "If Virginia had been too miserable to stand the life here, she wouldn't have done away with herself. She would have run off with some other man. Or perhaps gone back to the stage—which is just an indirect way of doing the same thing."

"You're not very charitable," murmured Vance.

"Charitable?" She laughed unpleasantly. "Perhaps not. But, at any rate, I'm not altogether stupid, either."

"Suppose," remarked Vance mildly, "that I should tell you that we found a suicide note?"

The girl's eyes opened wide, and she gazed at Vance in consternation.

"I don't believe it!" she said vehemently.

"And yet, Miss Llewellyn, it's quite true," Vance told her with quiet gravity.

For several moments no one spoke. Amelia Llewellyn's eyes drifted from Vance out into space; her lips tightened; and a shrewd, hard expression appeared on her face. Vance watched her closely, without seeming to do so. At length she moved in her chair and said with artificial simplicity:

"One never can tell, can one? I guess I'm not a very good psychologist. I can't imagine Virginia killing herself. It's most theatrical, however. Did Lynn attempt self-annihilation, too?—a suicide pact, or something of the sort?"

"If he did," returned Vance casually, "he evidently failed—according to the latest report."

"That would be quite in keeping with his character," the girl remarked in a dead tone. "Lynn is not the soul of efficiency. He always just misses the mark. Too much maternal supervision, perhaps."

Vance was annoyed by her attitude.

"We'll let that phase of the matter drop for the moment," he said with a new sharpness. "We're interested just now in facts. Can you tell us anything of your uncle's—that is, Mr. Kinkaid's—attitude toward your sister-in-law? The note we found mentioned that he had been particularly kind to her."

"That's true." The girl assumed a less supercili-

ous air. "Uncle Dick always seemed to have a soft
spot in his heart for Virginia. Maybe he felt that,
as Lynn's wife, she was to be pitied. Or maybe he
considered her an adventurer like himself. In any
event, there seemed to be a bond of some kind between
them. Sometimes I've thought that Uncle Dick has
let Lynn win at the Casino occasionally so that Virginia would have more spending money."

"That's most interestin'." Vance lighted a fresh
cigarette and went on. "And that brings me to another question. I do hope you won't mind. It's a bit
personal, don't y' know; but the answer may help us
no end. . . ."

"Don't apologize," the girl put in. "I'm not in
the least secretive. Ask me anything you care to."

"That's very sportin' of you," murmured Vance.
"The fact is, we should like to know the exact financial status of the members of your family."

"Is that all?" She looked genuinely surprised, perhaps even disappointed. "The answer is quite simple. When my grandfather, Amos Kinkaid, died, he
left the bulk of his fortune to my mother. He had
great faith in her business ability; but he didn't think
so much of Uncle Dick and willed him only a small
portion of the estate. We children—Lynn and I—
were too young to receive any individual consideration; and anyway, he probably counted on mother to
look out for our welfare. The result is that Uncle

Dick has had to look after himself more or less, and that mother is the custodian of Old Amos's money. Lynn and I are both wholly dependent on her generosity; but she gives us a fair enough allowance. . . . And that's about all there is to it."

"But how," asked Vance, "will the estate be distributed in the event of your mother's death?"

"That only mother can tell you," replied the girl. "But I imagine it will be divided between Lynn and myself—with the greater part, of course, going to Lynn."

"What of your uncle?"

"Oh, mother regards him with too much disapproval. I doubt seriously that she has considered him in her will at all."

"But in the event that your mother outlives both you and your brother, where would the money go then?"

"To Uncle Dick, I guess—if he were alive. Mother has a pronounced clannish instinct. She'd much prefer Uncle Dick to inherit the fortune to having it fall into the hands of an outsider."

"But suppose either you or your brother should die before your mother, do you think the remaining child would inherit everything?"

Amelia Llewellyn nodded.

"That is my opinion," she answered, with quiet frankness. "But no one can tell what plans or ideas mother has. And, naturally, it's not a subject that's ever discussed between us."

"Oh, quite—quite." Vance smoked for a moment and then raised himself a little in his chair. "There's one other question I'd like to ask you. You've been very generous, don't y' know. The situation is quite serious at the moment, and there's no tellin' what facts or suggestions may prove of assistance to us. . . ."

"I think I understand." The girl spoke with an apparent softness and appreciation of which I had heretofore thought her incapable. "Please don't hesitate to ask me anything that may be of help to you. I'm terribly upset—really. I didn't care for Virginia, but—after all—a death like hers is—well, something you wouldn't wish for your worst enemy."

Vance took his eyes from the girl and contemplated the tip of his cigarette. I tried to probe his mental reaction at the moment, but his face showed nothing of what was going through his mind.

"My question concerns Mrs. Lynn Llewellyn," he said. "It's simply this: if she had survived both you and your brother, what effect would that have had on your mother's will?"

Amelia Llewellyn pondered the question.

"I really couldn't say," she replied at length. "I've never thought of the situation in that light. But I'm inclined to believe mother would have made Virginia her chief beneficiary. She would probably have clutched at anything to keep Uncle Dick from getting the estate. And furthermore her almost pathological devotion to Lynn would affect her decision. After all, Virginia was Lynn's wife; and Lynn and everything pertaining to him has always come first with mother." She looked up appealingly. "I wish I could help you more than I have."

Vance rose.

"You have helped us no end—really. We're all gropin' about in the dark just now. And we sha'n't keep you up any longer. . . . But we'd like to speak to your mother. Would you mind asking her to come here to the drawing-room?"

"Oh, no." The girl rose wearily and went toward the door. "She'll be delighted, I'm sure. Her one ambition in life is to have a hand in every one's affairs and to be the centre of every disturbance." She went slowly from the room, and we could hear her ascending the stairs.

"A strange creature," Vance commented, as if he were thinking out loud. "A combination of extremes . . . cold as steel, yet highly emotional. Constant cerebral antagonism goin' on . . . can't make up her mind. She's livin' on a psychic borderline—heart and mind at odds. . . . Curiously symbolic of this entire case. No compasses and no way of takin' our bearin's." He looked up wistfully. "Don't you feel that, Markham? There are a dozen roads to take—and they all may lead us astray. But there's a hidden alley somewhere, and that's the route we have to take. . . ."

He walked toward the rear of the drawing-room.

"In the meantime," he said, in a lighter tone, "I'll indulge my zeal for thoroughness."

Behind heavy velour drapes in the middle of the rear wall were massive sliding doors; and Vance drew one of them aside. He felt along the wall in the room beyond, and in a few seconds there was a flood of light revealing a small library. We could see Vance stand for a moment looking about him; and then he went to the low kidney-shaped desk and sat down. On the desk stood a typewriter, and after inserting a piece of paper in it, he began typing. In a few moments he withdrew the paper from the machine, looked at it closely, and, folding it, put it in his inside breast pocket.

On his way back to the drawing-room he paused before a set of book-shelves and let his eye run over the neat array of volumes it held. He was still inspecting the books when Mrs. Llewellyn came in with an air of imperious regality. Vance must have heard her enter, for he turned immediately, and rejoined us in the drawing-room.

He bowed, and, indicating one of the large silk-covered chairs by the centre-table, asked her to sit down.

"What did you gentlemen wish to see me about?" Mrs. Llewellyn asked, without making any move to seat herself.

"I notice, madam," Vance returned, ignoring both her manner and her question, "that you have a most interestin' collection of medical books in the little room beyond." He moved his hand in a designating gesture toward the sliding doors.

Mrs. Llewellyn hesitated and then said:

"I shouldn't be in the least surprised. My late husband, though not a doctor, was greatly interested in medical research. He wrote occasionally for some of the scientific journals."

"There are," continued Vance, without any change of intonation, "several standard works on toxicology among the more general treatises."

The woman thrust out her chin aggressively, and, with the suggestion of a shrug, sat down with rigid dignity on the edge of a straight chair near the door.

"It's quite likely," she replied. "Do you consider them as having any bearing on the tragedy that has happened tonight?" There was an undercurrent of contempt in the question.

Vance did not pursue the subject. Instead, he asked her:

"Do you know of any reason why your daughter-in-law should have taken her own life?"

Not a muscle of the woman's face moved for several moments; but her eyes suddenly darkened, as if in thought. Presently she raised her head.

"Suicide?" There was a repressed animation in her voice. "I hadn't thought of her death in that light, but now that you make the suggestion, I can see that such an explanation would not be illogical." She nodded slowly. "Virginia was most unhappy here. She did not fit into her new environment, and several times she said to me that she wished she were dead. But I attached no importance to the remark, —it's a much abused figure of speech. However, I did everything I could to make the poor child happy."

"A tryin' situation," murmured Vance sympathetically. "By the by, madam, would you mind telling us—wholly in confidence, I assure you—what the general terms of your will might be?"

The woman glared at Vance in angry consternation.

"I *would* mind—most emphatically! Indeed, I resent the question. My will is a matter that concerns no one but myself. It could have no bearing whatever on the present hideous predicament."

"I'm not entirely convinced of that," returned Vance mildly. "There is one line of reasoning, for example, that might lead us to speculate on the possibility that one of the potential beneficiaries would gain by the—shall we say, absence?—of certain other heirs."

The woman sprang to her feet and stood in tense rigidity, her eyes glowering at Vance with vindictive animosity.

"Are you intimating, sir,"—her voice was cold and venemous—"that my brother——?"

"My dear Mrs. Llewellyn!" Vance remonstrated sharply. "I had no one in mind. But you do not seem to appreciate the significance of the fact that two members of your household have been poisoned tonight, and that it is our duty to ascertain every possible factor that may, even remotely, have some bearing on the case."

"But you yourself," protested the woman in a mollified voice, reseating herself, "advanced the possibility of Virginia's having committed suicide."

"Hardly that, madam," Vance corrected her. "I merely asked you whether you considered such a theory plausible. . . . On the other hand, do you think it likely that your son attempted to take his own life?"

"No—certainly not!" she replied dogmatically. Then a distracted look came into her eyes. "And yet . . . I don't know—I can't tell. He has always been very emotional—very temperamental. The least little thing would upset him. He brooded, and exaggerated. . . ."

"Personally," said Vance, "I cannot believe that your son attempted to end his life. I was watching him at the time he was stricken. He was winning heavily, and was intent on every turn of the wheel."

The woman seemed to have lost interest in everything but her son's welfare.

"Do you think he's all right?" she asked pleadingly. "You should have let me go to him. Couldn't you inquire again how he is?"

Vance rose immediately and went toward the door. "I'll be glad to, madam."

A few moments later we heard him talking over the telephone in the hall. Then he returned to the drawing-room.

"Mr. Llewellyn," he reported, "is apparently out of danger. Doctor Rogers has left the hospital; but the house physician on night duty tells me your son is resting quietly, and that his pulse is practically normal now. He believes Mr. Llewellyn will be able to return home tomorrow morning."

"Thank God!" The woman breathed a sigh of relief. "I shall be able to sleep now. . . . Was there anything more you wished to ask me?"

Vance inclined his head.

"The question will doubtless seem irrelevant to

you; but the answer may clarify a certain phase of this unfortunate situation." He looked directly at Mrs. Llewellyn. "Just what is Mr. Bloodgood's status in this household?"

The woman raised her eyebrows, and gazed back at Vance for a full half-minute before answering. Then she spoke in a conventional and curiously detached tone.

"Mr. Bloodgood is a very close friend of my son's. They were at college together. And I believe he knew Virginia quite well for several years before her marriage into our family. My brother—Mr. Kinkaid—has, for a long time, been an ardent admirer of Mr. Bloodgood's. He saw possibilities in the young man, and trained him for his present position. Mr. Bloodgood comes here to my home a great deal, both socially and on business. . . . You see," she added in explanation, "my brother lives here. The house is really half his."

"Just where are Mr. Kinkaid's quarters?" Vance asked.

"He occupies the entire third floor."

"And may I," continued Vance, "ask what the relationship is between Mr. Bloodgood and your daughter?"

The woman shot Vance a quick look, but did not hesitate to answer the question with apparent frankness.

"Mr. Bloodgood is deeply interested in Amelia. He has asked her to marry him, I believe; but she has given him no definite answer, as far as I know. Sometimes I think she likes him, but there are other times when she treats him abominably. I have a feeling she does not altogether trust him. But then again, she is constantly thinking of her art; and she may merely have the idea that marriage would interfere with her career."

"Would you approve of the union?" Vance asked casually.

"I'd neither approve nor disapprove," she said, and closed her lips tightly.

Vance regarded her with a slightly puzzled frown.

"Is Doctor Kane also interested in your daughter?"

"Oh, yes, I imagine he's interested enough—in a calf-like way. But I can assure you Amelia has no sentimental leanings in his direction. She uses him constantly though,—she has no scruples in that respect. Allan Kane is a great convenience to her at times; and he comes of a very good family."

Vance got up lazily from his chair and bowed.

"We sha'n't detain you any longer," he said with an air of stern courtesy. "We appreciate your help, and we wish you to know that everything will be taken care of with the least possible inconvenience to yourself."

Mrs. Llewellyn drew herself up haughtily, rose, and went from the room without a word.

When she was out of hearing Markham got to his feet aggressively and confronted Vance.

"I've had enough of this." His tone was one of irritable reproach. "All this domestic gossip is getting us nowhere. You're simply manufacturing bugaboos."

Vance sighed resignedly.

"Ah, well! Let's toddle along. The witchin' hour has long since passed."

As we went out into the hall, Detective Sullivan came down the stairs.

"The Sergeant's going to wait for the buggy and put everybody to bed," he told Markham. "I'm going home and hit the hay. Good night, Chief. . . . So long, Mr. Vance." And he lumbered out into the night.

The cadaverous butler, looking tired and drowsy, helped us with our coats.

"You'll take orders from Sergeant Heath," Markham instructed him.

The man bowed and went toward the door to open it for us. But before he reached it there came the sound of a key being inserted in the lock; and in another moment Kinkaid blustered into the hall. He drew up shortly as he caught sight of us.

"What's the meaning of this?" he demanded truculently. "And what are those officers doing outside?"

"We're here on a matter of duty," Markham told him. "There's been a tragedy here tonight."

The muscles of Kinkaid's face suddenly relaxed into a calm, cold, blank expression: he had become, in the fraction of a second, the inscrutable gambler.

"Your nephew's wife is dead," Vance said. "She was poisoned. And, as you know, Lynn Llewellyn also was poisoned tonight. . . ."

"To hell with Lynn!" Kinkaid spoke through his teeth. "What's the rest of the story?"

"That's all we know at the moment—except that Mrs. Llewellyn died at approximately the same time her husband collapsed in your Casino. The Medical Examiner says belladonna. Sergeant Heath of the Homicide Bureau is waiting upstairs for the car to take her body to the mortuary. We hope to know more after the *post mortem* tomorrow. Your nephew, by the by,—according to the latest report—is out of danger. . . ."

At this moment there came a startling interruption. A woman's voice cried out from somewhere upstairs. A door opened and slammed, and a faint sound of moaning came to us. Then there was the sound of heavy footsteps running along the hallway above us. The blood seemed to freeze in my veins—

I cannot say why—and we all moved toward the stairs.

Suddenly Heath appeared on the upper landing. Under the strong glare of the hall light I could see that his eyes were round with excitement. He beckoned to us with an agitated sweep of the arm.

"Come up here, Mr. Markham," he called in a husky voice. "Something—something's happened!"

CHAPTER VII

MORE POISON

(Sunday, October 16; 3:30 a. m.)

When we reached the upper landing Heath was already far down the hall, lumbering toward the open door of a room at the north end. We followed rapidly, but the Sergeant's broad back obstructed our view, and it was not until we had actually entered the room that we saw the cause of the sudden and startling summons that had come to us. This room, like the hallway, was brilliantly lighted: it was obviously Mrs. Anthony Llewellyn's bedroom. Though larger than Virginia Llewellyn's room, it contained far less furniture,—there was a rigorous, almost bleak, severity about it, which reflected the character and personality of its occupant.

Mrs. Llewellyn stood leaning against the wall just inside the door, her lace handkerchief pressed tight against her drawn face, her eyes staring down at the floor in frightened horror. She was moaning and trembling, and did not lift her eyes when we came in. What she was looking at seemed to hold her fascinated and speechless.

There, within a few feet of her, limp and crumpled on the deep blue carpet, lay the still form of Amelia Llewellyn.

At first Mrs. Llewellyn merely pointed. Then with a great effort she said in an awed, husky voice:

"She was just going to her room, and she suddenly staggered, put her hands to her head, and collapsed there." Again she pointed stiffly to her daughter, almost as if she imagined we could not see the prostrate figure.

Vance was already on his knees beside the girl. He felt her pulse, listened to her breathing, looked at her eyes. Then he beckoned to Heath and motioned to the bed opposite. They lifted the girl and placed her across the bed, letting her head hang down over the side.

"Smelling salts," ordered Vance. "And, Sergeant, call the butler."

Mrs. Llewellyn jerked herself into activity, went to her dressing-table and produced a green bottle like the one that Kinkaid had given Vance at the Casino earlier that night.

"Hold it under her nose—not too close to burn," he instructed the woman, and turned toward the door.

The butler appeared. His weariness seemed to have vanished; he was now nervously alert.

"Get Doctor Kane on the phone," Vance said peremptorily.

The man went swiftly to a small telephone desk and began dialing a number.

Kinkaid remained in the doorway looking on with a hard face, rigidly immobile. Only his eyes moved as he took in each aspect of the situation. He looked toward the bed, but his gaze was not on the quiet form of his niece: it was coldly focused on his sister.

"What's the answer, Mr. Vance?" he asked stiffly.

"Poison," Vance mumbled, lighting a cigarette. "Yes—quite. Same like Lynn Llewellyn. An ugly business." He glanced up slowly. "Does it surprise you?"

Kinkaid's eyes drooped menacingly.

"What the hell do you mean by that question?"

But Doctor Kane was on the wire, and Vance spoke to him:

"Amelia Llewellyn's seriously ill. Come over immediately. And bring your hypo—caffein and digitalis and adrenalin. Understand? . . . Right-o." He replaced the receiver and turned back to the room. "Kane's still up, fortunately—he'll be here in a few minutes." Then he adjusted his monocle and studied Kinkaid. "What's your answer to my question?"

Kinkaid began to bluster, apparently thought better of it, and thrust out his jaw.

"Yes!" he snapped, meeting Vance's gaze squarely. "I'm as much surprised as you are."

"You'd be amazed to know how far I am from being surprised," Vance murmured, and moved to-

ward the two women. He took the smelling salts
from Mrs. Llewellyn, and again felt the girl's pulse.
Then he sat down on the edge of the bed and waved
Mrs. Llewellyn aside.

"What's the whole story?" he asked her, not un-
kindly. "Let's have it before the doctor gets here."

The woman had stumbled to a chair, seated herself
erectly, and drawn her robe about her. When she
spoke it was in a calm self-possessed tone.

"Amelia came to my room here and told me you
wanted to see me. She sat down in this chair I'm
sitting in now. She told me she'd wait for me here—
that she wanted to talk to me. . . ."

"Is that all?" asked Vance. "You didn't come
down immediately, don't y' know. I did a bit of typing in the interim."

Mrs. Llewellyn compressed her lips. She added
coldly:

"If it's essential for you to know: I put some powder on my face and straightened my hair at the dressing-table there. I delayed—to pull myself together.
. . . I knew it would be an ordeal."

"And durin' this spiritual preparation, just what
was your daughter doing or saying?"

"She didn't say anything. She lighted a cigarette
and smoked. . . ."

"Nothing else? No other indication of activity?"

"She may have crossed her knees or folded her

hands—I wasn't noticing." The woman spoke with withering sarcasm; then added: "Oh, yes. She leaned over to the night-table and poured herself a glass of water from the jug."

Vance inclined his head.

"Natural impulse. Nervous, upset. Too many cigarettes. Dry throat. Yes. Quite in order. . . ." He rose and inspected the vacuum-jug on the night-table between the bed and the chair in which Mrs. Llewellyn was sitting.

"Empty," he remarked. "Very thirsty. Yes. Or perhaps. . . ." He returned to his seat on the edge of the bed and appeared to meditate. "Empty," he repeated, and nodded thoughtfully. "Dashed funny. All water bottles empty tonight. At the Casino. In Mrs. Lynn Llewellyn's room. And now here. Great paucity of water. . . ." He looked up quickly. "Where, Mrs. Llewellyn, is the entrance to your daughter's room?"

"The door at the end of the little corridor that leads off the hall at the head of the stairs." She was inspecting Vance with a curious concern in which was mingled a patent antagonism.

Vance addressed himself to Heath.

"Sergeant, take a peep at the water-service in Miss Llewellyn's room."

Heath went out with alacrity. A few minutes later he returned.

"It's empty," he reported in stolid bewilderment.

Vance rose and, walking to an ash-tray on the telephone desk, put out his cigarette. He lingered dreamily over the process.

"Yes, yes. Of course. It would be. As I was sayin'. A drought hereabouts. Water, water nowhere; but many drops to drink—what? Reversin' the Ancient Mariner. . . . " He lifted his head and faced Mrs. Llewellyn again. "Who fills the jugs?"

"The maid—naturally."

"When?"

"After dinner—when she turns down the beds."

"Ever failed you before?"

"Never. Annie's thoroughly competent and dependable."

"Well, well. We'll speak to Annie in the morning. Matter of routine. In the meantime, Mrs. Llewellyn, please continue. Your daughter lit a cigarette, poured herself a glass of water, and you graciously answered our summons. Then, when you came back?"

"Amelia was still sitting in this chair." The woman had not moved her eyes from Vance. "She was still smoking. But she complained of a severe headache over her eyes, and her face was greatly flushed. She said her whole head throbbed and that there was a ringing in her ears. She also said she felt dizzy and weak. I attached no importance to it: I put it all down to nervous excitement, and told her she'd better go to bed. She said she thought she would—that she felt miserable—and then she spoke a little incoherently about Virginia, and got up. She pressed her hands to her temples and started toward the door. She was almost there when she swayed from side to side, and fell to the floor. I went to her, shook her, and spoke to her. Then I think I screamed,— horrible things seemed to be happening tonight and I was unstrung for a moment. This gentleman"— she indicated Heath—"came in and immediately called the rest of you. That's all I can tell you."

"That's quite enough," murmured Vance. "Many thanks. You've explained a good deal. Perfect description of your son's collapse, too. Quite. Parallel. Only he went out on the west side of the city—your daughter on the east side. He was harder hit. Shallower breathing, faster pulse. But same symptoms. He's pulled through nicely. Your daughter will come out of it even better, once she has some medical treatment. . . ."

He slowly drew out his cigarette-case and carefully selected a *Régie*. When it was lighted he sent a perfect blue ring toward the ceiling.

"I wonder who'll be disappointed by the recovery. I wonder. . . . Interestin' situation. Interestin' but tragic. Tragic no end." He lapsed into gloomy thought.

Kinkaid had moved into the room, and now sat gingerly on the edge of the heavy fumed-oak centre-table.

"You're sure it's poison?" he asked, his fish-like eyes fixed on Vance.

"Poison? Yes, yes. Excitation symptoms, of course. But that won't do. Collapse, or faint, from natural causes, responds to an inverted head and smellin' salts. This is different. Same here as with your nephew. One difference, though. Lynn got the bigger dose."

Kinkaid's face was like a mask, and when he spoke again his lips scarcely moved.

"And like a damned fool I gave him a drink from my carafe."

Vance nodded.

"Yes. I noticed that. Grave blunder on your part —speakin' *ex post facto*."

The butler appeared at the door again.

"Pardon me, sir." He spoke directly to Vance. "I trust you will not think me presumptuous. I heard your inquiry regarding the water jugs, and I took it upon myself to waken Annie and ask her regarding them. She assured me, sir, she filled them all tonight, as usual, when she did the rooms shortly after dinner."

Vance looked at the gaunt, pallid man with open admiration.

"Excellent, Smith!" he exclaimed. "We're most grateful."

"Thank you, sir."

The sound of a bell came to us. The butler hastened away, and a few moments later Doctor Kane, still in dinner clothes and carrying a small medicine case, was ushered in. His color was even paler than when I had last seen him, and there were shadows under his eyes. He went directly to the bed where Amelia Llewellyn lay unconscious. There was a look of distress on his face that struck me as a personal rather than a professional one.

"Symptoms of collapse," Vance told him, standing at his side. "Thin, fast pulse, shallow breathing, pallor, *et cetera*. Drastic stimulants indicated. Caffein first—three grains,—then digitalis. Maybe the adrenalin won't be needed. . . . Don't ask questions, doctor. Work fast. My responsibility. Been through it once tonight already."

Kane followed Vance's instructions. I felt a bit sorry for him, though at the time I could not have explained my attitude. He impressed me as a pathetic character, a weakling dominated by Vance's stronger personality.

While Kane was in the bathroom preparing the hypodermic, Vance prepared Amelia Llewellyn's arm for the injection. When the caffein had been administered, Vance turned to us.

"We'd better wait downstairs."

"Are you including me?" Mrs. Llewellyn asked haughtily.

"It might be best," said Vance.

The woman acquiesced ungraciously, preceding us to the door.

A little while later Doctor Kane joined us in the drawing-room.

"She's reacted," he told Vance in a voice that was somewhat tremulous with emotion. "Her pulse is better and her color is more normal. She's moving a little and trying to talk."

Vance rose.

"Excellent. . . . You put her to bed, Mrs. Llewellyn. . . . And you, doctor, please hover round a while and watch things." He moved toward the door. "We'll be back in the morning."

As we were going out, the wagon arrived to take away the body of Virginia Llewellyn. The drizzle had ceased, but the night was still damp and cold.

"Distressin' case," Vance commented to Markham, as he started the motor of his car and headed downtown. "Devilish work goin' on. Three persons poisoned—one of 'em quite dead; the two others under medical care. Who'll be next? Why are we here, Markham? Why is anything? And all eternity to dawdle about in. Depressin' thought. However. . . ." He sighed. "There's a great darkness. I can't find my way. Too many obstacles thrown in our path, clutterin' up the road. Lies and realities all shuffled together—and only one way open to us—the way of make-believe, leadin' to the worst crime of all. . . ."

"I don't get your meaning." Markham was gloomy and perturbed. "Naturally I feel some sinister influence——"

"Oh, it's far worse than that," Vance interjected. "What I was tryin' to say is that this case is a crime within a crime: *we* are supposed to commit the final horror. The ultimate chord in this macabre symphony is to be our conviction of an innocent person. The entire technique is based on a colossal deception. We are supposed to follow the specious and apparent truth—and it will not be the truth at all, but the worst and most diabolical lie of the whole subtle business."

"You're taking it too seriously." Markham endeavored to be matter-of-fact. "After all, both Lynn Llewellyn and his sister are recovering."

"Yes, yes." Vance nodded glumly, not taking his eyes from the shining macadam of the roadway. "There's been a miscalculation. Which merely makes it all so much more difficult to figure out."

"It happens, however——" began Markham; but Vance interrupted impatiently.

"My dear fellow! That's the damnable part of it. 'It happens.' Everything 'happens'. There's no design. Chaos everywhere. It happens that Kane prescribed rhinitis tablets containing the drug that gives the exact symptoms of Virginia Llewellyn's hideous death. It happens that Amelia Llewellyn was in the clothes closet at just the right moment to hear Virginia cry out and to witness her passing. It happens that Lynn Llewellyn and his wife were poisoned at practically the same moment, though they were on different sides of the city. It happens that Amelia drank the water in her mother's jug. It happens that every one was in the house tonight at dinner-time and thus had access to all the bathrooms and water-services. It happens that no water was in any of the carafes when we got to them. It happens that Kinkaid gave Lynn a drink from his carafe ten minutes before the chap collapsed. It happens that I received a letter and was on hand to witness Lynn's passing out. It happens that Doctor Kane was invited to dinner at the last moment. It happens that we were in the house when Amelia was poisoned. It happens that Kinkaid arrived at the house at just that moment. It happens the letter I received was postmarked Closter, New Jersey. It happens——"

"Just a moment, Vance. What's the point of that last remark about Closter?"

"Merely that Kinkaid has a hunting lodge on the outskirts of Closter and spends much of his time there, though I believe he closes it for the season before this time of year—generally in September."

"Good Heavens, Vance!" Markham sat up straight and leaned forward. "You're not intimating——"

"My dear fellow—oh, my dear fellow!" Vance spoke reprovingly. "I'm not intimating anything: just driftin' along vaguely in what the psychoanalysts call free association. . . . The only point I'm endeavorin' to make is that life is real and life is earnest, and that there's nothing real and nothing earnest about this case. It's tragic—fiendishly tragic —but it's a drama of puppets; and they're all being manipulated in a carefully prepared stage set—for the sole purpose of deception."

"It's the devil's own work," mumbled Markham hopelessly.

"Oh, quite. A clear case of Luciferian guilt. A soothin' idea. But quite futile."

"At least," submitted Markham, "you can eliminate Lynn Llewellyn's wife from the plot. Her suicide——"

"Oh, my word!" Vance shook his head. "Her death is the subtlest, most incalculable part of the plot. Really, y' know, Markham, it wasn't suicide. No woman, in the circumstances, commits self-destruction that way. She was an actress and vain,—Amelia explained that to us in no uncertain terms. Would she have made herself unlovely, with a generous ap-

plication of skin food and a hair-net, for her last
great dramatic scene on earth? Oh, no, Markham.
No. She had gone to bed in the most approved conventional and slovenly domestic fashion, with all indications of having looked forward to the morrow—
unpleasant as it might have turned out to be. . . .
And why should she have called out in distress when
the poison began to work?"

"But the note she left," Markham protested.
"That was certainly indicatory enough."

"That note would have been more convincing,"
Vance answered, "if it had been more in evidence. But
it was hidden, so to speak—folded and placed under
the telephone. *We*, d' ye see, were supposed to find
it. But *she* was to die without knowing of its existence."

Markham was silent, and Vance continued after a
pause.

"But we were not to believe it. That's the incredible part of it. We were to suspect it—to look for
the person who might have prepared it and put it
there for us."

"Good God, Vance!" Markham's voice was
scarcely audible above the hum of the car. "What
an astounding idea!"

"Don't you see, Markham?" (Vance had drawn
up sharply in front of Markham's house.) "That
note and the letter I received were typed in precisely

the same inexpert way—obviously both of them were done by the same person: even the punctuation and the margination are the same. Do you think for one moment a distracted woman on the point of suicide would have sent me the letter I received? . . . And that reminds me. . . ."

He reached into his pocket and, taking out the letter, the suicide note, and the sheet of paper on which he had typed a few lines in the Llewellyn home, handed them to Markham.

"I say, will you have these checked for me? Get one of your bright young men to use his magnifying glass and scientific tests. I'd adore an official verification that all were done on the same machine."

Markham took the papers.

"That's easy," he said, and looked at Vance with questioning uncertainty. Then he got out of the car and stood for a moment on the curb. "Have you anything in mind for tomorrow?"

"Oh, yes." Vance sighed. "Life has a way of going on here and there. Everything returneth. One generation passeth away, but the sun also ariseth. It's all vanity and vexation of spirit."

"Pray abjure Ecclesiastes for the moment," Markham pleaded. "What about tomorrow?"

"I'll call for you at ten, and take you to the Llewellyn house. You should be there. Bounden duty and all that. Servant-of-the-people motif.

Sad. . . ." He spoke lightly, but there was a look
on his face that belied his tone. Markham, too, must
have seen it and recognized its significance. "I could
bear to have communion with Lynn and Amelia when
they will have recovered. A bit of research, don't y'
know. They're both survivors, as it were. Heroically
rescued by your *amicus curiæ*. Meanin' myself."

"Very well," acquiesced Markham with marked
discouragement. "Ten o'clock, then. But I don't see
just where questioning Lynn and Amelia Llewellyn
will get you."

"I don't ask to see the distant scene——"

"Yes, yes," grunted Markham. "One step enough
for you. I know, I know. Your Christian piety
augurs ill for somebody. . . . Good night. Go home.
I detest you."

"And a jolly old tut-tut to you."

The car sped dangerously down the slippery street
toward Sixth Avenue.

CHAPTER VIII

THE MEDICINE CABINET

(Sunday, October 16; 10 a. m.)

At exactly ten o'clock in the morning Vance stopped his car in front of Markham's apartment. The weather had cleared somewhat; but there was still a chill in the air, and the sky was overcast. Markham was waiting for us in the lobby. He was scowling and impatient, and there was a troubled look in his eyes. The morning papers had carried brief stories of Virginia Llewellyn's death, with lurid headlines. They quoted a short, non-committal statement by Heath, and gave a half-column of family history. Neither Lynn Llewellyn's poisoning at the Casino nor Amelia Llewellyn's collapse at her home was mentioned,—the Sergeant must have tactfully avoided any mention of these two occurrences. But the story was startling enough: the very absence of details gave it an added mystery and stimulated public speculation. Suicide was the explanation advanced, and the suicide note was stressed—although, according to the accounts, the police had not divulged its contents. Many pictures—of Virginia

Llewellyn, Mrs. Llewellyn and Kinkaid—accompanied the text. Markham carried the rumpled papers under his arm when he came out on the sidewalk.

"My dear Justinian!" Vance greeted him. "I'm amazed and delighted. You're actually up and about. And have you breakfasted too? Such touchin' devotion to your civic duties!"

"Furthermore," grumbled Markham in patent ill-humor, "I've roused one of our experts on this Sabbath morning and sent all those typewritten papers to the laboratory. Also I've routed Swacker * out of bed and told him to report at the office."

Vance wagged his head in derisive admiration.

"I'm positively staggered by your matutinal activities."

When we arrived at the Llewellyn house the door was opened for us by the butler. Heath was in the entrance hall, glum and officious. Snitkin and Sullivan were also there, smoking ponderously and looking bored.

"Anything new, Sergeant?" Markham asked.

"Call it new, if you like, sir." The Sergeant was irritable. "Three hours' sleep I've had, and the usual battle with the reporters. And nowhere to go from here. I've been hanging around waiting to hear from you." He shifted his cigar to the other side of his mouth. "Everybody's in the house. The old

* Swacker was Markham's secretary.

woman came downstairs at eight-thirty and shut herself up in that room with the books off the drawing-
room——"

Vance turned to him.

"Really, now! And how long did she tarry there?"

"About half an hour. Then she went back
upstairs."

"Any report on the young lady?"

"She's all right, I guess. She was walking around,
and I heard her talking. Young Doc Kane came in
half an hour ago. He's upstairs with her now."

"Have you seen Kinkaid this morning?"

Heath snorted.

"Sure, I've seen him. He came down bright and
early. Wanted to give me a drink, and said he was
going out. But I told him he'd have to stick around
till I got orders from the District Attorney."

"Did he object?" asked Vance.

"Hell, no. Said that was fine with him. Seemed
pleased. Said he could attend to everything by phone,
ordered a gin rickey, and went back upstairs."

"I'd rather have enjoyed hearing his phone calls,"
murmured Vance.

"It wouldn't have done you any good," Heath
told him, with a gesture of discouraged disgust. "I
listened in on the phone down here. He talked to his
broker at his home, and the fellow named Bloodgood, and the cashier at the Casino. All business
stuff. Not even a dame."

"No out-of-town calls?" Vance put the question casually.

Heath took the cigar from his mouth and gave him a shrewd look.

"Yeah—one. He called a Closter number——"

"Ah!"

"But he didn't get any answer, and hung up."

"That's very disappointin'," commented Vance. "Do you remember the number?"

Heath gave a broad triumphant grin.

"Sure. And I found out all about it. It's the old boy's hunting lodge just outside of Closter."

"Stout fella!" Vance nodded admiringly. "Anything else happen around here, Sergeant?"

"The young guy blew in about twenty minutes ago. . . ."

"Lynn Llewellyn?"

Heath nodded indifferently.

"He looked groggy, but he isn't what you'd call an invalid. Stepped lively and wanted to pick a fight with me and Snitkin." The Sergeant smiled sourly. "I guess he hadn't heard the news—though, from all the dope I've heard around here, he wouldn't give a damn, anyway. I didn't spill anything to him —I simply told him, nice and sweet, he'd better go up and talk to mother. . . . And that's everything exciting that's happened."

Vance shook his head sadly.

"You're not very helpful this morning, Sergeant. And I had hopes. However. . . ." He looked at Markham and sighed pensively. "We're doomed to the rôle of beavers, old dear—just toilin', busy beavers. We'll tackle Lynn and Amelia. But first I think I'll take another peep at Virginia's boudoir. Maybe we overlooked something last night." He went toward the stairs, and Markham and I followed.

As we approached the top landing the sound of a hysterical voice came to us from the direction of Virginia Llewellyn's room, though no words were distinguishable. But when we stepped into the upper hallway the whole tragic scene was revealed to us. Through the open door at the end of the corridor we could see Mrs. Llewellyn seated in a straight chair near the bed, and kneeling before her was Lynn Llewellyn. He was looking up at his mother excitedly and clutching her arms. The woman's head was bent forward and her hand was on his shoulder. They were both in profile, and apparently were not aware of our presence at the head of the stairs.

Lynn Llewellyn's high-pitched, sobbing voice now came to us distinctly.

". . . Darling, darling," he was crying, "tell me you didn't do it! Oh, God, tell me it wasn't you! You know I love you, dearest—but I wouldn't have wanted that! . . . You didn't do it, did you, mother? . . . " The agony in the man's voice sent a chill over me.

Vance cleared his throat emphatically to apprize them of our presence in the hall, and both of them turned their heads quickly toward us. Lynn Llewellyn swiftly rose to his feet and moved out of our range of vision. When we had walked down the hall and entered the room, he was standing at the north window, his back to us. Mrs. Llewellyn had not left her chair, but she had drawn herself up erectly, and she nodded with rigid formality as we stepped across the threshold.

"We are sorry to intrude, madam," Vance said, with a bow. "But from what Sergeant Heath told us, we expected to find this room unoccupied. Otherwise, we would have asked to be announced."

"It doesn't matter," the woman returned wearily. "My son wished to come here, for some morbid reason. He has just heard of his wife's death."

Lynn Llewellyn had turned from the window and now stood facing us. His eyes were blood-shot and the lids were red; and he was wiping away the evidence of recent tears.

"Excuse my condition, gentlemen," he apologized, with a bow of recognition toward Vance. "The news was a terrible shock. It—it upset me . . . and I'm not quite myself this morning, anyway."

"Yes, yes. We can understand that," Vance answered compassionately. "A tragic business. And I was at the Casino last night. That was a bad jolt you got. Your sister had a similar experience here last night. Glad you're both about."

Llewellyn nodded vaguely and looked around him with dazed eyes.

"I—I can't understand it," he mumbled.

"We're here to do what we can," Vance told him. "And we'll want to have a talk with you a little later. In the meantime would you mind waiting elsewhere? We've a few things to look into first."

"I'll wait in the drawing-room." He went heavily to the door, and as he passed his mother he paused and gave her a searching, appealing look which she returned with a cold meaningless stare.

When he had left the room Mrs. Llewellyn turned her eyes calculatingly toward Vance.

"Lynn," she said, with a twisted, mirthless smile, "has practically accused me of being responsible for the tragic events of this past night."

Vance nodded with understanding.

"I regret that we inadvertently overheard some of the things he said to you. But you must not forget, madam, that he may not be quite himself this morning."

The woman appeared not to have heard what Vance had said.

"Of course," she explained, "Lynn does not actually believe the terrible intimations beneath his words. The poor boy is suffering horribly. It has all been a great shock to him. He is reaching out blindly for some explanation. And he has a vague fear that perhaps I am responsible. I wish I could help him,—he is really suffering." Despite the deep concern indicated by her words, her voice had a harsh, artificial tone.

Vance regarded her a moment. His eyelids drooped over his cold gray eyes, giving him a lackadaisical expression.

"I quite understand your feelings," he said. "But why should your son suspect you?"

Mrs. Llewellyn hesitated before answering; then the muscles of her face stiffened as if with a sudden and distressing decision.

"I may as well tell you frankly that I was strongly opposed to his marriage. I did not like the girl—she was not worthy of him. And perhaps I have been too outspoken in my remarks to him; I fear now I have not sufficiently restrained my feelings in that regard. But I was unable to dissemble in a matter so vital to my son's happiness." She compressed her lips and then went on. "He may have misconstrued my attitude. He may have taken my remarks even more seriously than they were intended—overestimated the actual strength of my emotions."

Vance nodded discreetly.

"I see what you mean," he murmured. Then he added, without taking his gaze from the woman: "You and your son are unusually close to each other."

"Yes." She nodded with a somewhat abstracted glance. "He has always depended on me."

"A case of mother fixation, perhaps," suggested Vance.

"It might be that." She looked down at the floor and, after a moment, said: "It would, of course, account for his fears and suspicions regarding me."

Vance moved toward the mantel.

"Yes, that might be one explanation. But we sha'n't go into the possibility just now. Later, perhaps. In the meantime——"

The woman rose vigorously.

"I shall be in my own room—if you care to see me again." And she strode angrily to the door and closed it after her.

Vance studied the tip of his cigarette in lazy meditation.

"Now, what was the meanin' of all those intimate details? She was not in the least worried about herself, and actually seemed pleased that we had surprised the hysterical Lynn in his jittery genuflexion. I wonder. . . . Painful and perplexin', Markham." He raised his head and surveyed the room dreamily. "Let's see if we can find anything new. Anything at all. The slightest suggestion. The whole background of this case is beclouded. No suggestion of a color scheme. Really, Markham, I don't know anything. The mind is a total loss. Suspicious shadows, however. . . ."

He strolled to the dressing-table and looked over the array of cosmetics.

"The usual items," he murmured, opening the top drawer and peering in. "Yes—quite in keeping. Eye shadow, mascara, eyebrow pencil—all the accessories of vanity. And not used last night. Indicatin', as I said, an unexpected and not a premeditated demise." He closed the drawer and moved toward the mantel, pausing before a small hanging bookshelf. "All French novels of the cheaper variety. The lady had abominable liter'ry taste." He tested the old-fashioned china clock on the mantel. "Duly wound— and keeping excellent time." He leant over the grate. "Nothing," he complained dolefully. "Not even a cigarette butt." He moved on round the room, carefully observing each item of furniture and decoration, and finally came to a halt at the foot of the bed. "I fear there's nothing to help us here, Markham." He smoked despondently a moment, and then turned toward the rear of the room without enthusiasm. "The bathroom, once more," he sighed. "A mere precaution. . . ."

He went into the bathroom and spent some time

going over it and reinspecting the medicine cabinet. When he came back into the bedroom his eyes were troubled.

"Deuced queer," he muttered to no one in particular. Then he lifted his gaze to Markham. "I'd swear some one has been shifting some of those bottles around in the medicine cabinet since I looked at them last night."

Markham was unimpressed.

"What makes you think that?" he asked impatiently. "And, even if it were so, what would be the significance?"

"I can't answer both of your questions," Vance returned. "But last night I got a very definite picture of the—what shall I call it?—compositional outlines of the bottles and boxes and tubes in the cabinet—a certain balance of arrangement of the angles and intersecting planes such as one gets in a Picasso painting. And now the proportions and relationships of the lines and squares are not the same. There's a slight distortion of last night's values: it's as if some stress had been obliterated or some linear form had been accentuated,—the picture has been touched up or modified in some way. But apparently nothing is missing from the cabinet—I've checked every item." He drew deeply on his cigarette. "And yet there is some accent lacking or transposed—an added crayon mark or a small erasure somewhere."

"It sounds esoteric," grumbled Markham.

"I dare say," Vance agreed. "Probably is. Anyway, I don't at all like it. Disturbin' to my æsthetic sensibilities." He shrugged and went again to the head of the bed.

He stood for some time gazing down thoughtfully at the night-table, with its ash-tray, telephone and silk-shaded electric lamp. Then he slowly pulled out the little drawer.

"My word!" He suddenly reached into the drawer and took out a blue-steel revolver. "That wasn't there last night, Markham," he said. "Amazin'!" He inspected the revolver and, replacing it carefully exactly where he had found it, turned about.

Markham was more animated now.

"Are you sure it wasn't there last night, Vance?"

"Oh, yes. Yes. No error of vision."

"Even so," said Markham, with a look of baffled impatience, "what possible bearing can it have on all these poisonings?"

"I haven't the slightest idea," Vance admitted placidly. "But nevertheless, it's of academic interest. . . . Suppose we go downstairs and have parlance with the unhappy Lynn."

CHAPTER IX

A PAINFUL INTERVIEW

(Sunday, October 16; 10:30 a. m.)

When we entered the drawing-room Lynn Llewellyn was stretched out in a low comfortable chair, smoking a pipe. On seeing us he struggled to his feet with apparent effort and leaned heavily against the centre-table.

"What do you make of it?" he asked in a husky voice, his bleary eyes moving from one to the other of us.

"Nothing yet." Vance scarcely looked at the man and walked toward the front window. "We were hopin' you might assist us."

"Anything you want." Llewellyn moved his arm vaguely in a gesture of docile compliance. "But I don't see how I can help you. I don't even know what happened to me last night. Guess I was winning too much." His tone had become bitter, and there was a sarcastic sneer on his lips.

"How much did you win?" asked Vance casually and without turning.

"Over thirty thousand. My uncle told me this

morning he had it cached in the safe for me." The muscles in the man's jaw tightened. "But I wanted to break his damned bank."

"By the by,"—Vance came back toward the centre of the room and sat down by the table—"did you note any peculiar taste in the whisky or the water you drank last night?"

"No, I didn't." The answer came without hesitation. "I thought about that this morning—tried to recall—but there was nothing wrong as far as I could tell. . . . I was pretty much excited at the time, though," he added.

"Your sister drank a glass of water in your mother's room here last night," Vance went on, "and she collapsed with the same symptoms you showed."

Lynn Llewellyn nodded.

"I know. I can't figure it out. It's all a nightmare."

"Just that," agreed Vance. Then, after a pause, he glanced up. "I say, Mr. Llewellyn, has it occurred to you that your wife might have committed suicide?"

The man started sharply and, swinging round, glared at Vance with open-eyed astonishment.

"Suicide? Why—no, no. She had no reason——" He broke off suddenly. "But you never can tell," he resumed in a strained, repressed voice. "It may be, of course. I hadn't thought of it. . . . Do you really think it was suicide?"

"We found a note to that effect," Vance told him quietly.

Llewellyn said nothing for a moment. He took a few unsteady steps forward; then he walked back and sank into the chair in which we had found him.

"May I see it?" he asked at length.

"We haven't it here now." Vance spoke in an off-hand manner. "I'll show it to you later. It was type-written—addressed to you—and spoke of her unhappiness here, and of your uncle's kindness to her. And she wished you the best of luck at roulette. Brief—to the point—and final. Neatly folded under the telephone."

Llewellyn did not move. He gazed straight ahead without comment or any facial indication of what he was thinking. Finally Vance spoke again.

"Do you, by any chance, own a revolver, Mr. Llewellyn?" he asked.

The man stiffened in his chair and looked at Vance with quick interrogation.

"Yes, I own one. . . . But I don't see the point."

"And where do you generally keep it?"

"In the drawer of the night-stand by the bed. We've had a couple of bad burglar scares."

"It wasn't in the drawer last night."

"Naturally. The fact is, I had it with me." Llewellyn was still studying Vance with a puzzled frown.

"Do you always carry it with you when you go out?" Vance asked.

"No—rarely. But I do take it with me, as a rule, when I go to the Casino."

"Why do you single out the Casino for this peculiar distinction?"

Llewellyn paused before answering, and a look of smouldering animosity came into his eyes.

"I never know what may happen to me there," he said at length, between locked teeth. "There's no love lost between my uncle and myself. He'd like to get my money, and I'd like to get his. To be quite truthful with you: I don't trust him. And the events of last night may or may not justify my suspicions. At any rate, I have my theory as to what happened."

"We sha'n't ask to hear it just now, Mr. Llewellyn," Vance replied coldly. "I have my ideas too. No use confusin' the issue with speculations. . . . So you carried your revolver to the Casino last night and then replaced it in the night-table drawer this morning: is that correct?"

"Yes! That's exactly what I did." Llewellyn spoke with a show of aggressiveness.

Markham put a question.

"You have a permit to carry a gun?"

"Naturally." Llewellyn sank back in his chair.

Vance got up again and stood looking down at him.

"What about Bloodgood?" he asked. "Is he another reason for your fears?"

"I don't trust him any more than I do Kinkaid— if that's what you mean," the man returned unhesitatingly. "He's under Kinkaid's thumb—he'd do anything he was told to do. He's as cold as a fish, and he's got plenty to win if he could stack his cards the way he wants to."

Vance nodded understandingly.

"Yes—quite. I see your point. Your mother practically told us he wants to marry your sister."

"That's right. And why not? It would be a good catch for him."

"Your mother further told us your sister has repeatedly refused his offers of marriage."

"That doesn't mean a thing." There was an undertone of bitterness in his voice. "Her enthusiasm for art doesn't go very deep. She's just temporarily bored with life. She'll get over it. And she'll marry Bloodgood eventually. She likes him in her cold-blooded superficial way." He paused and then added with a sneer: "A good combination they'll make, those two."

"Illuminatin' comments," murmured Vance. "And young Doctor Kane? . ."

"Oh, he doesn't count. He's serious about Amelia, though, and he'll always be her slave. He's doomed for life to play *Cayley Drummle* to her *Paula Tanqueray*. She'd rather fancy it, too. Selfish as they come."

"A pathological household," commented Vance.

Llewellyn took no offense. He merely showed his teeth and said:

"That's just the word. Every one tangential to the norm. Like all old families with too much money and no object in life but to incubate hatred and hatch plots."

Vance looked at Llewellyn with vague, almost pathetic, curiosity.

"Do you know anything about poisons?" he asked unexpectedly.

The man chuckled unpleasantly: the question seemed to leave him entirely unimpressed.

"No," he said readily. "But there's evidently some one else around here who knows a hell of a lot about poisons."

"There are several fairly comprehensive volumes on the subject in the little library yonder," Vance remarked, with a casual wave of the hand.

"What!" Llewellyn started up. "Books on poison —here?" His eyes glared at Vance for a moment as if in surprised horror. Then he sank back and fumbled with his pipe.

"Does the fact astonish you?" Vance's voice was particularly mild.

"No, no; of course not," Llewellyn answered almost inaudibly. "For the moment perhaps—it brought things pretty close to home. Then I remembered my father's scientific interests . . . probably some of his old books. . . ."

A thoughtful frown had settled on Llewellyn's forehead: his eyes had narrowed to intense speculation. A train of unpleasant suspicions seemed to be running through his mind, and he held himself almost rigid.

Without appearing to do so, Vance watched him for several moments before speaking.

"That will be all for the present, Mr. Llewellyn," he said in polite dismissal. "You may go upstairs. If we need you further we'll notify you. You'd better stay in today and rest. Sorry to have upset you by mentioning the treatises on toxicology."

The man had risen and was already at the door.

"You didn't upset me exactly," he said, halting. "You see, Kane's a doctor, and Bloodgood took a degree in chemistry at college, and Kinkaid wrote a whole chapter on Oriental poisons in one of his travel books——"

"Yes, yes, I understand perfectly," Vance interrupted with a slight show of impatience. "They wouldn't have needed the aid of the books, of course. And if the books were used as source material for what happened yesterday, that might narrow the thing down to you and your mother and your sister. And you and your sister were both victims of the plot. So that leaves only your mother as the person who might have made use of the books. . . . Something like that went through your mind—eh, what?"

Llewellyn drew himself up aggressively.

"No, nothing of the kind!" he protested vigorously.

"My mistake," Vance muttered, with a curious note of sympathy in his voice. "By the by, Mr. Llewellyn, I meant to ask you: did you, by any chance, go to your medicine cabinet for any purpose this morning?"

The man shook his head thoughtfully.

"No-o. . . . I'm sure I didn't."

"It doesn't matter. Some one did." Vance returned to his chair, and Llewellyn, with a shrug, left us.

"What do you make of him, Vance?" Markham asked.

"He's sufferin'." Vance sighed meditatively. "Full of morbid ideas. And worryin' abominably over mama. Sad case. . . ."

"He said he had a theory about last night. Why didn't you urge him to expound it to us?"

"It would have been too painful, revealin' only his state of mind. Yes, too painful. I'm burstin' with sorrow, as it is. I cannot bear much more, Markham. I want to go far away. I want to bask in sunshine. I want to see Santa Claus. I want to eat some real English sole. I want to hear Beethoven's C-sharp minor quartet. . . ."

CHAPTER X

(Sunday, October 16; 11:15 a. m.)

Sergeant Heath appeared at the door.

"The young doc's just coming downstairs. Want to see him, sir?"

Vance hesitated; then nodded.

"Yes, ask him to come in here, Sergeant."

Heath disappeared and a moment later Doctor Kane entered the drawing-room. His face was drawn and haggard as if from insufficient rest, but the look of strain and apprehension had gone from his eyes. His manner was almost cheerful as he greeted us.

"How is your patient this morning?" Vance asked him.

"Practically normal, sir. I remained here a couple of hours after you gentlemen went last night, and Miss Llewellyn was resting quietly when I left. Naturally she feels weak this morning and is highly nervous; but her pulse and respiration and blood-pressure are normal."

"Have you any suggestion, doctor," Vance asked,

157

"as to what drug it was that brought about her condition last night?"

Doctor Kane pursed his lips and looked into space.

"No," he returned at length, "—though I've naturally thought about the matter a good deal. Her symptoms were the usual ones of collapse—nothing distinctive about them—and, of course, there are a number of drugs that, therapeutically speaking, could have produced them. An overdose of any one of the various proprietary sleeping powders containing the barbiturates might have done it. But, you can understand, I shouldn't care to express an opinion offhand. I had intended to do a little research on the subject as soon as I return to my office."

Vance did not push the subject. He let the doctor go and then sent for the butler.

Smith was as imperturbable as ever, and his face was still pale.

"Please tell Miss Llewellyn," Vance said, "that we should like to have a few words with her, either in her own quarters or here in the drawing-room—whichever is more convenient for her."

The butler bowed and went out. On returning he informed Vance that Miss Llewellyn would see us in her room, and we went upstairs.

The girl was reclining on a chaise-longue, dressed in elaborately embroidered Japanese pyjamas. At her side stood a small red-lacquered tabouret on which were a complete cigarette service, a few art magazines, and a silver statuette of abstract design in imitation of Archipenko. Her greeting to us was a curt nod and a cynical attempt at a smile.

"Your visit, I understand from Doctor Kane, just missed coming under the head of 'viewing the remains.' "

"We are delighted," Vance returned seriously, "to find you so much better."

"But some one," she said bitterly, "surely will not take my recovery in so charitable a light." She shrugged slightly and made a grimace. "I'm beginning to feel like a visitor at the Borgias' palace. I was positively afraid to take my toast and coffee this morning."

Vance nodded understandingly.

"I doubt, though, that you need have any further fear. Something went radically wrong last night. The poisoner must have lost his way among unforeseen coincidences. And by the time he has reassembled his lines and planned another campaign of action, we hope to have the situation well in hand. We at least know now where we must look for indicat'ry activities."

Amelia Llewellyn glanced up quizzically and all cynicism faded from her face.

"That sounds," she remarked, "as if you knew more than you are divulging."

"Yes—quite. Considerably more. But not enough. Still, we're forrader, and always hoping. . . . You've seen your brother? He's quite recovered. And he got an uglier jolt than you did."

"Yes," the girl mused. "We're the two failures. It's quite like us, you know. We're always disappointing somebody."

"I trust," said Vance, "I sha'n't disappoint you in this case. In the meanwhile would you mind if I took a peep in your clothes closet and made a little experiment there?"

"Peep and experiment, by all means. I'd be delighted." She waved her arm almost gayly toward a door at her left.

Vance went to it and opened it. The space beyond was, as she had explained to us the night before, an old-fashioned passageway which had connected the two main rooms in the south wing of the house. There was a shoe-rack and a small cupboard on the right, and on the left hung a long row of dresses and gowns. Halfway down the passage there still remained the old marble-topped washbasin with its two high swan-necked spigots. At the opposite end of the improvised closet another door was visible. Vance walked to it and opened it, and we could see through into the large bedroom where Virginia Llewellyn had met her tragic end.

Vance came back to us and, turning to me, said:

"Van, go into the other room, close both doors and

stand beside the bed. Then call to me in a fairly loud voice. When you hear me knock on the farther door, call again in the same tone of voice."

I went through the clothes closet into the farther room and, standing beside the bed on which Virginia Llewellyn had died, called out. After a few moments I heard Vance's knock on the door, and I called again. Then Vance opened the door.

"That's all, Van. Many thanks."

When we were again in Amelia Llewellyn's room, the girl gave Vance a satirical look.

"And what, Monsieur Lecoq," she asked, "did you learn?"

"Merely that you told us the ⁺ruth regarding the acoustic possibilities between the two rooms," Vance returned lightly. "I could not hear Mr. Van Dine with both doors shut, but I did hear him distinctly while standing in the clothes closet."

The girl drew a deep dramatic sigh.

"I'm so glad to have my veracity proved for once. Mother's favorite criticism of me is that I would always rather lie than tell the truth."

"Speaking of your mother"—Vance sat down and regarded the girl with serious eyes—"I want you to tell us just how you came to drink the glass of water in your mother's room last night."

Amelia Llewellyn sobered quickly under Vance's grave tone.

"How does one ever come to take a drink of water?

—I only know that I felt thirsty and instinctively reached for the water that stood at my side. I was going to wait there until mother came back. I was naturally upset and wanted to talk to some one——"

"Did you taste anything peculiar about the water?"

"No. It seemed perfectly all right."

"How much water was in the jug?"

"Barely a glassful. I vaguely remember wishing there had been more. But I was too lazy to get up. When mother returned I had a raging headache and my ears were pounding, and I felt terribly weak. My mind was confused, and I started for my own room. That's all I recall."

"You distinctly remember your mother's return to the room?"

"Oh, yes. We said something to each other—I don't recall just what it was. I probably complained about my headache—but everything was spinning around by that time."

"When you first felt thirsty—that is, before you took the drink of water—did you mention the fact to your mother?"

The girl thought a moment. Then she answered:

"No. Mother was at the dressing-table, beautifying herself for the interview with you. I don't think we spoke to each other then. I merely reached over and helped myself to what water there was in the jug, and mother swept grandly and haughtily from the room."

"What of the water in your own carafe last night?" Vance asked. "The maid said she filled it. But while you were unconscious in your mother's room, your carafe was inspected and found to be empty."

"Yes, I know it was empty. I drank all the water it contained while I was sketching earlier in the night." Her eyes opened a little wider. "Was my water poisoned too?"

Vance shook his head.

"No, it couldn't have been. Too much time elapsed after you had taken it. You would have felt the effects of the poison within half an hour, at the most. . . ."

Vance turned suddenly and went softly to the hall door. He turned the knob carefully and then swiftly drew the door inward. In the corridor, facing us, stood Richard Kinkaid.

Not a muscle of his face moved to show that Vance's sudden action had disconcerted him. He took his cigarette slowly from his mouth and bowed with curt formality.

"Good morning, Mr. Vance," he said in a cold steady voice. "I came down to inquire about my niece. But when I heard voices in the room I thought you and Mr. Markham might be here, and I didn't

care to disturb you. But you evidently heard
me. . . ."

"Yes, yes. I heard some one moving outside the
door." Vance stood to one side. "We were just asking Miss Llewellyn a few questions. But we're
through now. . . . She is much better this morning."

Kinkaid stepped into the room, and, after greeting his niece with a conventional phrase or two, he sat
down.

"Any further developments?" he asked, lifting his
head to Vance with a shrewd, calculating look.

"Oh, any number," Vance returned non-committally. "We're bringin' in the sheaves, as it were.
But we're not rejoicin' just yet. . . . However, I'm
glad you dropped in. I wanted to ask you, before we
went, for Bloodgood's address. We're particularly
anxious to have a little chat with the gentleman."

Kinkaid's jaw tightened, and the look in his eyes
became harder. But there was no other indication
that he was surprised by Vance's remarks.

"Bloodgood lives at the Astoria Hotel in 22nd
Street," he said, and slowly broke the ashes of his
cigarette in a tray at his side. "However," he added,
with a slight note of contempt in his voice, "you're
barking up the wrong tree there. But go ahead and
question him, by all means. He'll be at his hotel all
day—I just talked to him on the phone. But you'll
be wasting your time—Bloodgood's as straight as
a die."

"I really don't know the chap very well," Vance murmured. "But in view of the fact that it was he who ordered the plain water for Lynn Llewellyn last night at the Casino, it might be interestin' to have his views on the subject, don't y' know."

Amelia Llewellyn, who had perceptibly stiffened at the mention of Bloodgood's name, now stood up and stared at Vance defiantly, with blazing eyes.

"What do you mean by that?" she demanded. "Are you accusing Mr. Bloodgood of giving the poison to Lynn?"

"My dear young lady!"

"For if you are," the girl went on in a cold angry tone, "I can tell you exactly who's responsible for everything that happened to this family last night."

Vance gazed at her calmly, and the chill of his tone matched hers.

"When the truth becomes known, Miss Llewellyn," he said, "your testimony will not, I fear, be needed." He bowed formally to her and to Kinkaid, and we took our departure.

When we were about to descend to the main floor Vance hesitated and then went down the hall toward Mrs. Llewellyn's room.

"There's one little matter I should like to mention to the lady of the house before we go," he explained to Markham, as he tapped on the door.

Mrs. Llewellyn received us with ill grace, and her manner was one of marked antagonism.

Vance apologized for disturbing her.

"I merely wished to tell you, as a matter of possible interest to you, that your son seemed greatly perturbed when I informed him of the volumes on toxicology in the library downstairs. He appeared to have been unaware of their existence."

"And how should that be of interest to me?" the woman retorted with frigid disdain. "My son does not read much—his literary needs are entirely satisfied by the theatre. I doubt if he is familiar with the titles of any of the books his father left. Nothing could be more alien to his interests than scientific research. And his perturbation over the existence of books on poisons in this house is, I assure you, perfectly natural in view of the experience through which he went last night."

Vance nodded as if satisfied with the explanation.

"That's quite plausible," he murmured. "And perhaps you can give us as colorable an explanation as to why you yourself spent part of this morning in the library."

"So my movements are being spied upon!" This was said with scathing and vindictive indignation; but a change quickly came over the woman's attitude. Her eyes contracted and a shrewd smile appeared on her lips. "The intimation beneath your words is, I suppose, that I myself was consulting these particular books on poisons."

Vance waited, and the woman went on.

"Well, that's exactly what I was doing. If it will help your inquiries: I was looking for some common drug that might account for the condition of my son and daughter last night."

"And did you find any reference to such a drug, madam?"

"No! I did not."

Vance left the matter there. He made his adieux and added:

"There will be no more spying—for the time being, at least. The police will be removed from your house, and you and your family are free to come and go as you please."

When we were again downstairs Markham drew Vance into the drawing-room.

"See here, Vance," he asked with deep concern, "aren't you being a bit hasty?"

"My dear Markham," Vance chided him, "I'm never hasty. Slow and ploddin' and cautious. The human tortoise. I must have reasons for everything I do. And I now have excellent reasons for temporarily removing all supervision from the Llewellyn domicile."

"Still," demurred Markham, "I don't like the situation here, and I think it should be watched."

"A virtuous idea. But not helpful." Vance contemplated Markham plaintively. "Watching won't

help us. I was invited to watch Lynn's passing out.
And we were all in the house watching last night
when Amelia was smitten. Really, y' know, we can't
be expected to supply every member of the Llewellyn
family with a bodyguard indefinitely."

Markham studied Vance closely, as if trying to
read the other's thoughts.

"That was a peculiar remark of the girl's about
her knowing who's responsible for this affair. Do
you believe her, perhaps?"

"Oh, my dear Markham!" Vance sighed dolefully.
"It's too early to begin believing anybody. Our only
hope lies in complete skepticism. Honest doubtin'—
not thought highly of, but most efficacious at times.
It gives the mind a chance for free functioning."

"Nevertheless," pursued Markham irritably, "you
have something definite in mind when you want the
police withdrawn."

"No, no; nothing definite," Vance returned, and
smiled. "Just gropin'. Strainin' for illumination.
. . . And I do want to see the *post-mortem* report.
That, at least, will be definite. It may even prove
revealin'."

Markham gave in reluctantly.

"Very well. I'll give Heath orders to withdraw
temporarily and send the boys home."

"And tell him to pick up our croupier at the Astoria
and bring him along to your office," said Vance. "I'm
eager to grill him, as you public prosecutors would

say. And I think the judicial and depressin' surroundings of the Criminal Courts Building might
have the right psychological effect."

"What do you expect to find out from him?"

"Nothing—positively nothing," Vance replied,
and then added: "But even negation might be of
help. I have a psychic feelin' this case will eventually
be solved by minus signs."

Markham grunted, and we went out into the hall
where the Sergeant was waiting despondently.

Ten minutes later Vance and Markham and I were
on our way downtown, Heath having been duly instructed as to the procedure Vance had requested.

As soon as we entered the District Attorney's
dingy but spacious old office overlooking the drab
gray walls of the Tombs, Markham rang for Swacker
and inquired about the statement from Doctor Doremus and also about the report on the specimens of
typing which had been sent to the scientific laboratory.

"The lab report has come in," Swacker told him,
pointing to a sealed envelop on the desk; "but Doctor Doremus phoned at eleven to say that the autopsy
report is delayed. I called back ten minutes ago, and
one of the assistants told me the report was on the
way. I'll bring it in as soon as it arrives."

Markham jerked his head curtly, and Swacker
went out.

"Delayed—eh, what?" drawled Vance. "There

shouldn't have been any trouble. Belladonna poisoning indicated. The toxicologist knew just what to look for. I wonder. . . . In the meantime, let's see what the bright boy with the magnifying glass has to offer."

Markham had already opened the envelop to which Swacker had referred. He laid the three specimens of typing to one side and perused the accompanying report. After a few moments he put that down too.

"Just what you suspected," he said to Vance without enthusiasm. "All the typing was done on the same machine, and within a reasonable period of time—that is, the ink on the ribbon was at the same stage of usage in all three, and it can't be stated with certainty which of the three was typed first. Also, the suicide note and the letter you received were probably typed by the same person. Peculiarities of pressure and punctuation, and consistencies in the errors when the wrong letters were struck, are the same in both. There's a lot of technical detail, but that's the gist of it." He picked up the report and held it out to Vance. "Do you care to see it?"

Vance made a negative gesture with his hand.

"No, I merely craved verification."

Markham leant forward.

"See here, Vance, what's the point about these two typewritten documents? Granting the possibility that the girl did not commit suicide, what would have been the object of the person who poisoned her in sending you that letter?"

Vance became serious.

"Really, Markham, I don't know." He walked slowly up and down the room as he spoke. "If only that letter to me and the suicide note had been typed by two different people, the thing would be comparatively simple. It would merely mean that some one had planned to poison the girl in such a way as to make it appear as suicide, and that some one else, with an inkling that murder was afoot, had sent me a dramatic call for help. In such an event two conclusions might have been tenable: first, that the anonymous letter-writer feared that Lynn was to be the victim; and, second, that the writer suspected Lynn himself of having murderous designs on his wife and wanted me to keep an eye on him. . . ."

"And they were both victims," Markham interpolated glumly. "So that hypothesis doesn't get us anywhere. In any event, it's merely a speculation based on the false premise that two different people prepared the two documents. Why not come to the point?"

"Oh, my dear chap!" Vance moaned. "I'm strivin' desperately to come to the point—but, dash it all! I don't know what the point is. As the case stands now, the poisoner deliberately called my attention to the situation and even intimated strongly that Lynn's wife was not going to commit suicide, but would actually be murdered."

"That doesn't make sense."

"And yet, Markham, you have the substantiation of my apparently insane conclusion lying on your desk. There's the suicide note; there's the letter to me, filled with innuendoes and suspicions of foul play; and there's your report that the same hand typed them both."

He paused.

"And what of the next inevitable step in our ratiocination? As I have whispered into your reluctant ear, I think the murderer wishes us to look in the wrong direction for our culprit. He is, as it were, attempting the impossible feat of taking two tricks of the same suit with a singleton. And that's what makes the thing so subtle and fiendish."

"But it wasn't a singleton," Markham objected. "You overlook the fact that *three* people were poisoned. If your theory is correct, why couldn't the murderer merely have poisoned the girl and then poisoned the victim we were supposed to fix on? Why make us a party to his plan when he's apparently in the wholesale poisoning business?"

"A reasonable question," Vance nodded; "and one that has tortured me since last night. Such a procedure would have been the rational one. But, Mark-

ham, there's nothing rational about this crime.
There isn't merely one straw-man confronting us,
but a series of straw-men. And I have a horrible suspicion that they are arranged in a circle, with the
actual murderer beyond the circumference. Our only
hope lies in the fact that something has gone wrong.
In any delicate and intricate mechanism, one little
failure—one trifling slip in functioning—under-
mines the entire structure and renders the machine
incapable of operating. This is not a plastic crime.
Despite all its hyper-subtleties and divagations and
convolutions, it's static and fixed in its conception.
And therein lies both its strength and its weakness. . . ."

At this point Swacker tapped on the leather
swinging door and pushed it open. In his hand was
a thick envelop.

"The autopsy report," he said, placing it on
Markham's desk and going out again.

Markham opened the envelop at once and glanced
over the typewritten pages which were bound together in a blue folder. As he read, his face clouded
and a puzzled look came into his eyes; and when he
had reached the end of the last page there was a deep
scowl on his forehead.

He raised his head slowly and fixed on Vance, who
had seated himself before the desk, a look of baffled
calculation.

"My dear Markham," Vance complained; "what dark secret are you hoarding?"

"There was no belladonna whatever found in the girl's stomach! And no quinin or camphor—which entirely eliminates the rhinitis tablets."

Vance lighted a cigarette with slow deliberation.

"Any details?"

Markham referred to the report.

"The exact findings are: Congestion of the lungs; considerable serum in the pleural cavities; blood mostly in the veinous side of the circulation; right heart engorged, left heart comparatively empty; brain tissues and meninges congested; and the throat, trachea and œsophagus hyperemic. . . ."

"All symptoms of death from asphyxia." Vance looked out unhappily through the high windows to the south. "And no poison! . . . Does Doremus offer any opinion?"

"Nothing specific," Markham informed him. "He's professionally non-committal here. He merely states that the cause of asphyxia is as yet unknown."

"Yes, yes. Pending analysis of the liver, kidneys, intestines, and blood. That will take a couple of days. But some of the poison should be in the stomach, if it was taken orally."

"But Doremus states here that the history he received of the case and his findings on the immediate examination of the body, indicated an overdose of belladonna or atropin."

"We knew that last night." Vance reached over and, taking the report, went through it carefully. "Yes. As you say."

He settled down in his chair, brought his eyes slowly back to Markham's troubled gaze, and took a deep inhalation on his cigarette. Then he tossed the report back on Markham's desk with a despondent gesture.

"That tears it, old dear. A lady is given poison, presumably orally; but no traces of it are found. Two other persons are poisoned and recover. We are supposed to tag some innocent bystander for the heinous crime. . . . Oh, my aunt! What an astonishin' situation! . . ."

CHAPTER XI

FEAR OF WATER

(Sunday, October 16; 12:30 p. m.)

Swacker looked in.

"Sergeant Heath's here with a gentleman named Bloodgood."

Markham glanced at Vance, who nodded, and told Swacker to show them in.

Bloodgood was in an unpleasant and sullen mood. A brown cigarette hung limply from his thick lips, and his hands were thrust deep in his trousers pockets. He nodded stolidly to Vance, without speaking, and barely acknowledged his introduction to Markham and myself. Slouching to the nearest chair, he sank into it heavily.

"Go ahead," he said indifferently. "Kinkaid phoned me you were going to put me on the carpet."

"Did he, now?" Vance was again gazing out of the high windows. "That's most interestin'. Did he warn you to be careful, or advise you what to say?"

Bloodgood bristled.

"No. Why should he? But he did say you had

linked me up with Lynn Llewellyn's mishap last night."

"You linked yourself up, Mr. Bloodgood," Vance returned mildly, without turning his eyes from the gray skies beyond the dull window-panes. "We merely thought you might have some explanation or suggestion that would help us to get to the bottom of this devilish business."

Vance's tone, though assured and stern, was not unfriendly; and Bloodgood was evidently impressed by it, for he straightened up a little in his chair and dropped his ill-natured manner. Indeed, when he spoke I was again conscious of the man's poise and urbanity.

"There's really nothing I can explain, Mr. Vance. You're referring, I assume, to my instructions to the Japanese boy to bring Llewellyn plain water. . . . That was an unfortunate coincidence. I was merely being polite to a guest of the Casino—all in the line of duty. Kinkaid's a stickler for that sort of thing. I knew Llewellyn never drinks charged water, and I'd heard him order plain water earlier in the evening. Most of the boys know his tastes, but Mori hasn't been with us very long. And I'll say this for Llewellyn: he doesn't drink much when he's at the Casino. He's probably read somewhere that you must keep your brain clear when gambling. As if it mattered!" Bloodgood gave a snort of contempt. "Luck

doesn't inquire into a man's mental state before striking."

"Quite so," murmured Vance. "And the law of
probabilities operates on the sober and the inebriated
alike. Yes. Wholly amoral. Consolin' thought. But
I say, was there no motive behind your *politesse* to
Llewellyn other than the desire to live up to your
employer's standard of punctilio?"

"A sinister motive?" Bloodgood asked resentfully,
becoming suddenly rigid.

"Really, y' know, I didn't specify." Vance was
smoking placidly. "Why put the least charitable
construction on my query? I trust the worm of con-
science doth not begnaw thy soul."

Bloodgood relaxed, and the suggestion of a weary
smile moved the corners of his mouth.

"I'll probably hang myself yet. I do a kindly act,
and the recipient all but dies. You hand me a knife,
and I pick it up by the blade." He shrugged. "The
fact is, I wouldn't ordinarily have interfered with
Llewellyn's beverages at the Casino—I'm not over-
fond of the man—but I felt a little sorry for him
last night. Kinkaid doesn't like him, and he's had
the worst possible luck playing roulette. He rarely
wins, and Kinkaid is inclined to gloat over the fact.
Last night he had a run of good luck; he'd already
won back a considerable amount of what he'd pre-
viously lost. Then he went to pieces—psychological

reaction, I imagine—got nervous and unbalanced, and began doing the most preposterous things— covering his bets and even betting against himself, taking the short end of every percentage. He couldn't have lasted much longer. He needed a drink, if ever a man did; and when I saw the charged water, which he wouldn't have touched, I felt a sort of human inclination to help him out. So I ordered the plain water. In one way it was a good turn: he passed out some thirty thousand ahead. But my kindness evidently got *me* in wrong."

"Yes, things are like that. One never knows, does one? A whimsical world. No accountin' for it." Vance spoke impersonally. "By the by, do you know where the water, which you so charitably ordered, came from?"

"From the bar, I suppose."

"Oh, no. No. Not the bar. Mori was shunted on his errand of mercy. The water came from Kinkaid's private carafe."

Bloodgood sat up straight, and his eyes opened wide.

Vance nodded.

"Yes. Kinkaid told Mori to fetch the water from his office. Too many people at the bar, he explained to me. Unnecess'ry delay. Thinkin' only of Llewellyn. Every one so considerate of his welfare last night. Guardian angels. All very sympathetic.

And then the ungrateful johnnie collapses with poison."

Bloodgood started to speak but quickly closed his lips, and, sinking back in his chair, looked straight ahead in gloomy silence.

After a short pause Vance crushed out his cigarette and turned his chair round so that he was facing Bloodgood.

"You know, of course," he asked, "of the death of Llewellyn's wife last night?"

Bloodgood nodded without shifting his eyes from their far-away focus.

"I saw the papers this morning."

"Do you believe it was suicide?"

Bloodgood jerked his head around and stared at Vance.

"Wasn't it? The papers said a suicide note was found. . . ."

"That's correct. Not entirely convincing, however."

"But she was quite capable of suicide," Bloodgood offered.

Vance did not pursue the point.

"I suppose," he said, "that Kinkaid told you over the phone that Miss Amelia Llewellyn also had a close call last night?"

Bloodgood leaped to his feet.

"What's that!" he exclaimed. "He said nothing

about Amelia. What happened?" The man seemed highly perturbed.

"She took a glass of water—in her mother's room—and passed out very much as her brother did. No serious damage, though. She's quite all right this morning—we've just come from there. No cause for worry. . . . Please sit down. There are one or two other matters I wish to ask you about."

Bloodgood resumed his seat with seeming reluctance.

"You're sure she's all right?"

"Yes—quite. You might drop around to see her when you leave here. I'm sure she'll welcome a visit from you. Kinkaid's there too. . . . And by the by, just what are your relations with Kinkaid, Mr. Bloodgood?"

The man hesitated and then said non-committally:

"Purely business." When Vance did not speak Bloodgood went on. "There's a certain feeling of friendship involved, of course. I feel very grateful toward Kinkaid. If it weren't for him I'd probably be teaching chemistry or mathematics at a third of the salary I'm getting at the Casino, and being bored to death doing it. He's exacting, but he's generous enough. I can't say that I wholly admire him, but he has many likeable qualities, and he has always played the game aboveboard with me." Bloodgood stopped a moment and then added with a faint smile: "I think he likes me—and that fact, of course, tends to prejudice me in his favor."

"Do you attach any significance to his having ordered the water for Llewellyn from his own carafe?"

The question seemed to disturb Bloodgood considerably. He shifted in his chair and took a deep breath before answering.

"I don't know. Damn it, man, you have me wondering. It might be sheer coincidence—it's like Kinkaid to do things spontaneously like that: he has a very decent streak in him. He takes his losses like a gentleman and never complains when he gets set back. I know he runs his games straight; and, to tell the truth, I can't picture the man feeding a customer knock-out drops because the game's going against the house. Especially his own nephew."

"There could possibly have been reasons other than Llewellyn's winning last night," suggested Vance.

Bloodgood considered this for some time.

"I see what you mean," he replied at length. "With Amelia and Lynn and Lynn's wife out of the way . . ." He broke off and shook his head. "No! That doesn't check with Kinkaid's character. A gun, perhaps, in an emergency—I happen to know he shot himself out of some bad scrapes in Africa. But not poison. That's a woman's weapon. For all his inbreeding and subtleties of nature, Kinkaid's not a sneak."

"Forthright—eh, what?"

"Yes, just that. Either forthright or inactive. He does a thing or he doesn't. No *finesse*, in the psychological sense. That's why he's a great poker player and is only indifferent at bridge. He once said to me: 'Any woman can master bridge, but only a man can play good poker.' He's cold and ruthless and utterly without fear; and he's as shrewd as Lucifer himself. He'd stop at nothing to gain his ends. But he'd always be in the open. You could trust him even if he was out to get you. . . . Poison? No. That doesn't fit."

Vance smoked a while dreamily.

"You're a chemist, Mr. Bloodgood," he said finally, "and you've been rather close to Kinkaid. Tell me: is he, too, by any chance, interested in chemistry?"

For the first time during the interview Bloodgood appeared ill at ease. He shot a searching glance at Vance and cleared his throat nervously.

"I can't say that he is." His tone was not wholly convincing. "That's a subject that lies entirely outside his activities and interests." He stopped, and then added: "If there was any money in chemistry, of course, Kinkaid might be interested in the matter from the angle of pure speculation."

"Well, well," murmured Vance. "Always on the lookout. Cravin' a lucrative opening, so to speak. Yes. That always goes with the gambling instinct."

"Kinkaid realizes," supplemented Bloodgood, "that his present set-up can't last indefinitely. A gambling casino, at best, is only a temporary source of income."

"Quite. Our hyper-moral civilization. Sad. . . . But let's dismiss Kinkaid for the moment. . . . Tell us what you know of the youthful Doctor Kane. He was at the Llewellyns' for dinner last night, y' know, and Miss Llewellyn called him when Lynn's wife was stricken."

Bloodgood's face clouded.

"I've seen very little of the man," he replied stiffly; "and then only at the Llewellyns'. I believe he is interested in Miss Llewellyn. Comes of good family and all that. He's always been pleasant enough; has a congenial personality, but strikes me as something of a weakling. I'll say this, too, about him, since you've asked me: he has impressed me as being somewhat shifty at times, as if he were adding up numbers before answering a straight question or voicing an opinion."

"The *arrière-pensée* at work," suggested Vance.

Bloodgood nodded.

"Yes. Rather effeminate in his mental processes. Maybe, however, it's only his snobbery and his constant endeavor to please—the ingratiating manner that young doctors cultivate."

"What sort of chap was Lynn Llewellyn when you knew him at college?"

"He was all right. Pretty regular, but inclined to be wild. He wasn't much of a student—barely got by. He was too devoted to his good times, and lacked any serious goal. But I've never held that against him: it wasn't altogether his fault. His mother has always coddled him. She'd forgive anything he did and then turn round and make it possible for him to do it again. But she had the good sense to keep her hands on the purse strings. That's why the fellow gambles—he admits it frankly."

"He has an idea," put in Vance in a casual matter-of-fact tone, "that his mother may have been responsible for the poisonings last night."

"Good Heavens! Really?" Bloodgood seemed inordinately astonished. He sat pondering for several moments. Then he said: "I can understand his attitude in a way, though. He himself used to refer to her as 'the noblest Roman dowager of them all.' And he wasn't far wrong. She was always the man of the family. She'd brook no interference with her plans from anybody."

"You're thinkin' of Agrippina?" asked Vance.

"Something like that." Bloodgood lapsed into silence again.

Vance got up, walked to the end of the room and back, and then stopped before Bloodgood.

"Mr. Bloodgood," he said, his eyes fixed lazily on the other, "three people were poisoned last night. One of them is dead; the two others have recovered. No poison was found in Mrs. Lynn Llewellyn's stomach. Two of the victims—Llewellyn and his sister—collapsed after taking a glass of water. And the water carafe at the dead woman's bedside was empty when we arrived——"

"Good God!" The exclamation was little more than a whisper, but it had the penetrating quality of utter horror. Bloodgood struggled to his feet. His face had suddenly gone pale, and his sunken eyes shone like two polished metal disks. His cigarette fell from his lips but he paid no attention to it. "What are you trying to tell me? All three were poisoned by water——"

"Why should that astound you so—even if it were true?" Vance asked in a steady, almost indifferent, voice, his calm searching gaze still on the man. "In fact, I was about to ask you, after having given you the details of last night's occurrences, whether you could suggest any explanation."

"No—no. None whatever." There was an unnatural timbre in Bloodgood's tone, and he was breathing as if with effort. "I—I was upset by the recurrence of the water, since I was the one who ordered it for Llewellyn."

Vance smiled coldly and took a step toward the man.

"That won't do, Mr. Bloodgood." There was a steely quality in his attitude and manner. "You'll have to find a better excuse for your emotional upheaval."

"But how can I, man, when it doesn't exist?" protested Bloodgood, fumbling in his pocket for another cigarette.

Vance went on relentlessly: "Item one: you were at the Llewellyn dinner last night, and had access to all the carafes in the house. Item two: the only carafe that we know positively wasn't poisoned, is Miss Llewellyn's. Item three: you have proposed marriage to Miss Llewellyn. Item four: you are a chemist. . . . And now consider these four items in the light of the fact that it was also you who ordered plain water for Llewellyn at the Casino. Have you anything to say?"

Bloodgood had drawn himself together while Vance spoke. He swallowed several times and moistened his lips with his tongue. His arms hung straight at his sides, and he gave the impression that every muscle in his body had gone taut. He lifted his head and looked squarely at Vance.

"I understand the situation perfectly," he said in a hollow, even voice. "Despite the fact that no poison has actually been put in evidence, I appear to have manœuvred the events of last night. I have no explanation to make. Nor have I anything further to say. You may take whatever action you choose. The table is wide open." He smiled inscrutably. "*Faites votre jeu, monsieur.*"

Vance studied the man without change of expression.

"I think I'll hold my chips for the next turn of the wheel, Mr. Bloodgood," he said. "The play isn't over, don't y' know. And I've a new system in mind." He nodded in formal dismissal and turned away. "You're free to visit Miss Llewellyn."

"I hope to God your new system is better than most," the man mumbled, and took his departure without another word.

Vance resumed his seat and, taking out another *Régie,* smoked a while in troubled meditation.

"Deuced queer, that chap," he ruminated. "He told me something highly important, but—dash it all!—I don't know what it is. He was quite rational and honest until I mentioned water. The idea of poison didn't upset him, but the idea of water did. A sort of psychic hydrophobia. Very puzzlin', Markham. . . . There's something in his mind—something vital to our understanding of this case. But there's no way to get him to talk. I know the type. He actually invited arrest rather than answer my queries. . . . Fear—that's what it was. He knew he was cornered, but he was also aware that we didn't know why he was cornered. A shrewd gambler. A rapid mental calculator and a percentage player."

Vance wagged his head dolefully.

"Not a consolin' thought. We're dealin' with subtleties, Markham; and we're blindfolded. Gropin' at nebulæ. But he told us something! And we'll have to find out what it is. It's the key. Let us hope. Onward and upward, old dear. *Spes fovet, et fore cras semper ait melius.*"

CHAPTER XII

VANCE TAKES A JOURNEY

(Sunday, October 16; 1:30 p. m.)

Vance rose rather deliberately and walked to the desk.

"Markham," he said, with unwonted seriousness, "there's only one way of attacking this problem. We must keep our eyes fixed on the known physical facts of the case and ignore everything that may tend to divert us. That's why I'm going to ask you now to put me in touch immediately with your official toxicologist."

Markham looked up with a frown.

"You mean today?"

"Yes." Vance spoke emphatically. "This afternoon, if possible."

"But it's Sunday, Vance," Markham demurred. "It may be impossible. . . . However, I'll see what can be done."

He rang for Swacker.

"See if you can locate Doctor Adolph Hildebrandt," he instructed the secretary when he appeared. "He has left the laboratory by this time. Try telephoning to his home."

Swacker went out.

"Hildebrandt's a good man," Markham told Vance. "One of the best in the country. He's the plodding German type, cautious and pontifical and highly academic. But he always seems to lumber through. Without him we'd never have got a conviction in the Waite and Sanford cases. . . . He may be at home now, and he may not. If this wasn't Sunday. . . . However——"

At this moment a buzzer rang and Markham answered the telephone on his desk. After a brief conversation he replaced the receiver.

"You're in luck, Vance. Hildebrandt's at home—he lives in West 84th Street—and he'll be in all afternoon. You heard what I told him: that we'll be around later."

"That may help," Vance murmured. "Or it may prove just a false scent. But there's no other starting point. . . . My word! I wish I knew what was on Bloodgood's mind. The case, alas! resolves itself into a guessing contest." He sighed and took a deep puff on his cigarette. "In the meantime, let's lift up our hearts. I know where the green-turtle soup and the Harvey's Shooting Sherry are excellent and where an *omelette aux rognons* is assembled with love and finesse. *Allons-y, mon vieux.* . . ."

We got into his car and he took us to a little French restaurant in West 72nd Street, near Riverside Drive.* After our frappéed *crème de menthe* we proceeded uptown to Doctor Hildebrandt's.

The doctor was a rotund man, completely bald, with a moon-shaped face, protruding ears and pale blue eyes at once somnolent and keen. He was attired in a shabby smoking-jacket, baggy trousers and a pair of flapping felt bedroom slippers. His soft shirt was open at the throat, and his heavy woolen socks, of the most fantastically colored design, lay in thick folds about his ankles. He was smoking an enormous wooden-stemmed meerschaum pipe which curved downward over his chest fully eighteen inches.

He answered our ring himself, and ushered us into a narrow, stuffy living-room crowded with eighteenth-century rococo furniture. Despite his gruff, somewhat aloof manner, he was pleasant and gracious, and he acknowledged Markham's presentation of Vance and me with grave courtesy.

Vance immediately broached the subject he had come to discuss.

"We are here, doctor," he said, "to ask you a few questions regarding poisons and their actions. We are confronted with a serious and apparently obscure

* This was the same restaurant to which Vance took us during the investigation of the Kennel murder case, and where he bored Markham almost to the point of distraction with a long dissertation on Scottish terrier characteristics, blood-lines and pedigrees.

problem in connection with the death of a Mrs. Llewellyn last night. . . ."

"Ah, yes." Doctor Hildebrandt took the pipe slowly from his mouth. "Doremus called me this morning and I was present at the autopsy. I made an analysis of the stomach for one of the belladonna group. But I didn't find anything. I'm making a complete chemical analysis of the other organs tomorrow."

"What we're particularly interested in," Vance went on, "is whether a poison could have been the cause of death and yet not be evident in an analysis; and also how the poison, in such a case, might have been administered."

Doctor Hildebrandt nodded ponderously.

"I may be able to help you. And, on the other hand, I may not. Toxicology is an elaborate and difficult science. There are still many phases of it that we know nothing about."

He returned the pipe to his mouth and puffed heavily on it for several moments, as if arranging his thoughts. Then he spoke in a didactic, classroom manner.

"You understand, of course, that poison, in the biological sense, does not exist in the body if the substance is entirely insoluble; for, in such a case, it resists absorption into the blood stream. The corollary is that the more soluble a substance the more readily it will be absorbed into the blood stream and so act upon the body."

"What of the dilution of a poison in water, doctor?" asked Vance.

"Water not only hastens the absorption of a poison, but generally augments its activity. However, in the case of a corrosive, water naturally reduces the toxic effect. But, on the other hand, the condition of the stomach must be taken into consideration in the case of all poisons taken by mouth. If there is food in the stomach at the time of ingestion, the absorption of the poison is delayed; but if there is no food in the stomach, absorption, as well as the action of the poison, takes place more quickly."

"In the Llewellyn case the stomach should have been relatively empty," Vance put in.

"It was. And we can assume that if a poison was absorbed through the stomach, there was a fairly prompt action."

"We believe we know the approximate time at which the poison was taken," said Vance, "but we are interested in having the time scientifically established."

Again Doctor Hildebrandt nodded.

"Yes, the time is most helpful in all cases where criminality is suspected. But the determination of the point is not easy, for, in such cases, we have no actual evidence as to how, or under what conditions, the poison was taken. The time of administration depends entirely on the type of poison taken and on the symptoms observed. Nearly all the common poisons act quickly, although I can recall several physiological exceptions in which the action of the poison was delayed for hours after ingestion. But, generally speaking, the symptoms of poisons taken by mouth appear within an hour. In most cases, if the stomach is empty, the symptoms appear within ten or fifteen minutes after the administration. This is particularly true in the case of belladonna, or atropin, poisoning."

"What," asked Vance, "of a poison that is taken orally and whose presence is nevertheless not found in the stomach later?"

Doctor Hildebrandt cleared his throat judicially.

"Such a condition might be encountered with any number of poisons taken by mouth. It would simply mean that the system had absorbed all of the poison taken into the stomach. But there would, of course, be deposits of the poison in the blood and the tissues. Unfortunately, in too many cases of criminal poisoning, only the stomach is given to the toxicologist for chemical examination. Findings from the stomach alone are inconclusive, for, as I say, the rapid absorption of the poison may have left no traces of it in that organ. Naturally, the toxicologist who is given only the stomach for examination may assume that whatever poison he finds there is what might be called a surplus of the poison which has actually been ingested and absorbed by the system. But this is certainly not direct proof. That is why the other organs of any person suspected of having died by poisoning should be chemically analyzed—the liver, the kidneys, the intestines, perhaps even the brain and spinal cord. When poison is taken into the system orally it is first absorbed through the stomach. Then it is circulated in the blood. And finally it is deposited in the tissues of the liver, kidneys and other organs. You understand, of course, that poisons may be introduced into the body in other ways than by mouth; and in such cases there would naturally be no traces of the poison in the stomach."

"Ah!" Vance leaned forward. "That is one of the things we wish to know. In view of the fact that Mrs. Llewellyn died within a very short time after taking the poison, and there were no traces of it found in her stomach, I wish to ask you by what means, other than by ingestion, this poison—presumably belladonna—might have been administered."

Doctor Hildebrandt looked off into space thoughtfully.

"It could have been administered parenterally— that is, by hypodermic direct into the blood stream. Or it might have been absorbed through the mucous membranes of the nose or through the conjunctivæ.

In either case there would, of course, be no traces found in the stomach."

Vance smoked for a moment meditatively. Finally he put another question.

"Is there no case in which poison may have been taken orally and produced death, and yet left no traces in any organ of the body?"

The doctor brought his eyes back and let them rest on Vance.

"There are poisons which, when absorbed by the body, have no chemical action on the blood; and there are others that are not turned into insoluble compounds when they come in contact with the tissues. Such poisons are quickly eliminated from the system. If a victim of poisoning lives a sufficiently long time after taking such a poison, all traces of the lethal drug may entirely disappear from the body. But there is no indication that such was the case with the Llewellyn woman. With her the violent symptoms of poisoning appeared shortly after induction; and, as I understand, there were no processes of elimination."

"But," pursued Vance, "even in cases where no poison is found in any organ, would there not be organic changes in the body which would indicate the nature of the poison taken?"

"In certain cases, yes." Doctor Hildebrandt's gaze again drifted into space. "Such indications, however, are very unreliable. You see, various types of diseases can produce effects on the organs similar to those produced by certain poisons. If, however, the lesions discovered are identical with those produced by a poison which the person is supposed to have received, then one may assume that the lesions are the result of the poison. On the other hand, certain cases have come under my own observation where it was definitely known that a specific poison was taken, and yet the organs did not show any of the lesions which one would ordinarily have expected to find. In the famous Heidelmeyer case, for instance, it was known that death was caused by arsenic; yet neither the stomach nor the intestines were irritated, and the mucous membrane was even paler than it would have been normally."

Vance smiled despondently and shook his head.

"Toxicology, I see, is not a science which one might call even remotely mathematical. Still, there must be some way of reaching a definite conclusion from a given set of conditions. For instance, even though no traces of poison were found in the system, is it not possible to determine, by a person's symptoms and *post-mortem* appearances, what poison was taken?"

"That," returned Doctor Hildebrandt, "is as much a medical problem as a toxicological one. However, I will say this: the symptoms of many diseases closely simulate the symptoms of certain types of poisoning. For example, the symptoms of gastro-enteritis, cholera morbus, ulceration of the duodenum, uremia and acute acidosis, are fairly well duplicated by the symptoms of poisoning by arsenic, aconite, antimony, digitalis, iodin, mercury, and the various corrosive acids and alkalies. The convulsions accompanying tetanus, epilepsy, puerperal eclampsia and meningitis, are also caused by camphor, cyanides and strychnin. Dilated pupils, which are present in diseases that produce optic atrophy or a weakness of the oculomotor nerve, also follow poisoning by the belladonna group, cocain, and gelsenium; whereas contraction of the pupil, such as is common in tabes, for instance, is likewise caused by opium, morphin and heroin. Opium, paraldehyde, carbon dioxide, hyoscin and the barbitals produce coma; but so do cerebral hemorrhage, epilepsy and brain injuries. The delirium we find in cases of organic brain diseases and nephritis may often be duplicated by the administration of atropin, cocain, Canabis indica, or hasheesh, and various other poisons. Nitrobenzene, anilin and opium and its derivatives, produce cyanosis; yet so do diseases of the cardiac and respiratory system. Paralysis follows the taking of cyanides and carbon monoxide, but it is also produced by brain tumor and apoplexy. Then there's the question of respiration. Opium gives a slow respiration, but so

do uremia and brain hemorrhage. And the belladonna group of poisons produce rapid respiration,
such as is normally found in hysteria and lesions of
the medulla oblongata."

"My word!" Vance smiled. "The farther we go,
the more remote infallibility becomes."

The doctor grinned broadly.

"You know Goethe, yes? *Eigentlich weiss man nur
wenn man wenig weiss; mit dcm Wissen wächst der
Zweifel.*"

"That's hardly helpful, though." Vance sighed.
"I want to know more, not less."

"Toxicology is not entirely a hopeless science," the
doctor answered good-naturedly. "If a poison is
found in the organs of a dead person, and the pa-
thology of the case corresponds accurately to the
symptoms produced by that poison, one is justified in
accepting as a fact that the person died of that
particular poison."

Vance nodded.

"Yes. I can see that. But, as I understand you,
the absence of any determinable poison in the organs
does not mean that death was not due to the actual
administration of poison. Now, is it possible that
poison could actually be in the organs analyzed and
yet resist detection by the chemical analyst?"

"Oh, yes. There are several toxic substances for
which chemistry has not yet found the means of determination. Furthermore, you must not overlook the

fact that there are poisons which, when they come in contact with certain chemicals in the human body, are converted into harmless substances which one would ordinarily expect to find in the body."

"Then it is possible to poison some one deliberately, without fear of leaving any trace of the method of murder?"

Doctor Hildebrandt inclined his head slightly.

"Yes, that is possible. If one could successfully introduce common sodium into the stomach——"

"Yes, I know," interrupted Vance. "But the perforation of the stomach walls by the combustion of sodium was not the sort of thing I had in mind. What I wanted to ask is this: are there actual poisonous substances which might produce death and yet leave no trace?"

"Yes, there are such poisons," Doctor Hildebrandt returned slowly, taking his pipe from his mouth again. "For instance, there are various vegetable poisons which neither produce a specific lesion nor are chemically identifiable. And certain organic poisons may be converted into constituents commonly present in the body. Moreover, certain volatile poisons can be entirely dissipated by the time the toxicologist gets the organs for examination.* I am

* Doctor Hildebrandt, in answering Vance's question, mentioned specifically several poisons which leave no trace in the human body, but I am purposely not recording them here. Modern medical scientists and toxicologists will know those referred to; and I deem it both unnecessary and unwise to make such dangerous knowledge public property.

not mentioning the mineral acids which might cause corrosion and be eliminated from the system before death sets in, as I understand this type of poison does not interest you."

"I was thinking particularly," said Vance, "of some poison easily obtained, that could be given in a glass of water without its presence being detected by the victim."

Doctor Hildebrandt considered this for a moment. Then he shook his head gravely.

"No-o. I'm afraid the drugs and chemicals I have in mind would not satisfy all the conditions you impose."

"Still, doctor," Vance persisted, "is it not possible that a new poison may have been discovered recently which would meet my hypothetical requirements?"

"Certainly, that is possible," the doctor admitted. "New poisons are constantly being discovered."

Vance was silent for a while; then he asked:

"Would a lethal dose of atropin or belladonna, in a glass of water, be easily detected by any one who drank the mixture?"

"Oh, yes. There would be a distinctly bitter taste to the water." The doctor turned his eyes lazily to Vance. "Have you reason to believe that the poison in the Llewellyn case was given in water?"

Vance hesitated before answering.

"We are still only speculating on that point. The

fact is, two persons besides Mrs. Llewellyn were poisoned last night, but they recovered. And both of them had taken a glass of water shortly before collapsing. And the carafe at Mrs. Llewellyn's bedside was empty when we arrived."

"I see," the doctor mumbled, nodding slowly. "Well, perhaps after my chemical analysis of the other organs tomorrow, I can tell you more."

Vance rose.

"I'm deeply grateful to you, doctor. There is nothing else I have in mind at the moment. The case just now seems pretty well obscured. By the by, when will your report be completed?"

Doctor Hildebrandt got up ponderously and accompanied us to the door.

"That's hard to say. I'll begin work the first thing in the morning, and if I have any luck, I may have the report by tomorrow night."

We took our leave and Vance drove us direct to his apartment. He was quiet and apparently absorbed in thought. Moreover, he appeared troubled, and Markham made no attempt at conversation until we had settled ourselves in the library. Currie came in and lighted a fire in the grate, and Vance ordered a service of *Napoléon* cognac. It was then that Markham put his first question to Vance since leaving the doctor's apartment.

"Did you learn anything—that is, did anything

new suggest itself to you during your interview with Hildebrandt?"

"Nothing definite," Vance replied unhappily. "That's the queer part of this case. I feel as though I were almost touching something vital, and then it eludes me. Several times this afternoon, as the doctor dissertated, I felt that he was telling me something that I needed to know—but I couldn't put my finger on it. Ah, Markham, if only I were psychic!"

He sighed and warmed his cognac between his hands, inspiring its fumes through the narrow opening of the large pot-bellied *inhalateur*.

"But there's one motif that runs all through the events of last night—the water motif."

Markham looked at him thoughtfully.

"I noticed that several of your questions were centred about that theme."

"Oh, yes. Yes. They would be, y' know. Water runs through every act of this devilish drama. Llewellyn orders a whisky and insists upon plain water; but he doesn't drink it when it's brought to him. Later Bloodgood orders it for him, and Kinkaid sends the boy to his office to get the water. Then Kinkaid himself wants a drink of water, and the carafe's empty; so he sends it to the bar to be filled. Virginia Llewellyn's carafe is empty when we arrive at the house. Amelia Llewellyn takes the last glass of water from her mother's carafe and collapses. Her own carafe is later found to be empty—though she explained that point. Then Bloodgood gets emotional and enters the silence at the mere mention of water. Everywhere we turn—water! 'Pon my soul, Markham, it's like some hideous charade. . . ."

"You think, perhaps, all these victims were poisoned through water?"

"If I thought that, the whole problem would be simple." Vance made a hopeless gesture with his hand. "But there's no main thread holding these various repetitions of water together. Lynn Llewellyn drank whisky as well as water. Virginia Llewellyn could, of course, have been poisoned by water; but if the poison she took was belladonna or atropin—as the *post-mortem* signs indicated—she would have tasted the poison and not emptied the entire carafe. The only one of the three victims who we can say, with any degree of certainty, was poisoned by water, is Amelia. But even she tasted nothing amiss; and she had emptied her own carafe earlier in the evening without any untoward effects. . . . It's deuced queer. It's as if water had deliberately been introduced into this case to lead us somewhere. Any murder planned as subtly as this one seems to have been planned, doesn't present a recurring sign-post at every turn unless it has been calculated. Some of it may be coincidence, of course. But not all. That couldn't be. And Bloodgood's perturbation at the mention of water. . . . We have a key, Markham. But—dash it all!—we can't find the door. . . ."

He made a despairing gesture.

"Water. What a silly notion. . . . If only it were something besides water! Water can't injure any one, unless one were submerged in it. Why water, Markham? . . . Two parts of hydrogen and one part of oxygen . . . simple, element'ry formula——"

Vance suddenly stopped speaking. His eyes were fixed before him, and automatically he set down his cognac glass. He leaned forward in his chair, and then he sprang to his feet.

"Oh, my aunt!" He swung round toward Markham. "Water isn't necess'rily H_2O. We're dealing here with the unknown. Subtleties." His eyelids drooped in speculation. "It could be, don't y' know. It may be we are supposed to take the water trail— for a reason. . . . We have a chemist, and a doctor, and a gambler-financier, and books on toxicology, and hatreds, and jealousies, and an Œdipus complex, and three cases of poisoning—and water everywhere. . . . I say, Markham, busy yourself with something for a while. Read, think, sleep, fidget, play solitaire —anything. Only, don't talk."

He turned swiftly and went to a section of his book-shelves where he kept his scientific journals and pamphlets. For half an hour he rummaged among them, pausing here and there to read some paragraph or glance through some article he had found. At length he replaced all the periodicals and documents and rang for Currie.

"Pack my bag," he directed when the old English butler appeared. "Overnight. Informal. And put it in the car. I'm drivin'."

Markham stood up and faced Vance.

"See here!" He showed his annoyance. "Where are you going, Vance?"

"I'm takin' a little trip," Vance returned, with an ingratiating smile. "I'm seekin' wisdom. The water trail beckons. I'll be back in the morning, either wiser or sadder—or both."

Markham looked at him for a moment.

"What have you in mind?" he asked.

"Perhaps only a fantastic dream, old dear," smiled Vance.

Markham knew Vance too well to attempt to elicit any further explanation from him at that moment.

"Is your destination also a secret?" he asked with modified irritation.

"Oh, no. No." Vance went to his desk and filled his cigarette-case. "No secret. . . . I'm going to Princeton."

Markham stared at him in amazement. Then he shrugged, and wagged his head mockingly.

"And you a Harvard man!"

CHAPTER XIII

AN AMAZING DISCOVERY

(Monday, October 17; 12 noon)

It was nearly noon the next day when Vance returned to New York. I was busily engaged on routine work when he came into the library, and he barely nodded to me as he passed through to the bedroom. I could plainly see, by his look of concentration and his eager movements, that something urgent was on his mind. A short while later he emerged in a gray Glen Urquhart plaid suit, a subdued green Homburg hat and heavy blucher shoes.

"It's a miserable day, Van," he remarked. "There's rain in the air, and we are going into the country. Put away your bookkeeping and come along. . . . But I must see Markham first. Phone his office that I'll be there in twenty minutes—there's a good fellow."

While I got in touch with the District Attorney's office, Vance rang for Currie and gave instructions regarding dinner.

Markham was alone when we arrived at the Criminal Courts Building.

"I've held up my appointments waiting for you," he greeted Vance. "What's the report?"

"My dear Markham—oh, my dear Markham!" protested Vance, sinking into a chair. "Must I make a report?" He became serious and looked thoughtfully at Markham. "The fact is, I have practically nothing to report. A very disappointin' trip."

"Why did you go to Princeton at all?" Markham asked.

"To visit an old acquaintance of mine," Vance returned. "Doctor Hugh Stott Taylor—one of the great chemists of our day. He's the Chairman of the Department of Chemistry at the University. . . . I spent a couple of hours with him last night, inspecting the Frick Chemical Laborat'ry."

"Just a general tour of inspection?" Markham asked, watching Vance shrewdly. "Or something specific?"

"No. Not general." Vance inhaled on his cigarette. "Quite specific. I was interested, d' ye see, in heavy water."

"Heavy water!" Markham sat bolt upright in his chair. "I've come across a reference somewhere to heavy water——"

"Yes—yes. Of course. There has been considerable about it in the papers. Amazin' discovery. One of the great events in modern chemistry. Fascinatin' subject."

He lay back in his chair and stretched his legs out before him.

"Heavy water is a compound in which the hydrogen atom weighs twice as much as the hydrogen atom in ordin'ry water. It's really a liquid in which at least ninety per cent of the molecules consist of oxygen combined with the recently discovered heavy hydrogen. The formula is H^2H^2O, though it is now generally referred to scientifically as D_2O. The interestin' thing about it is that it looks and tastes like ordin'ry water. Actually, there is about one part of heavy water in five thousand parts of ordin'ry water; but because of the loss in the process of extraction, it comes nearer to requiring ten thousand parts of plain water to produce one part of the heavy water. In certain laborat'ries they have treated as much as three hundred gallons of ordin'ry water to produce one ounce of heavy water. The actual discovery of heavy water was made by Doctor Harold C. Urey of Columbia University. But a large part of the practical research in this new and amazin' compound has been done by the scientists at Princeton. The apparatus in the Frick Chemical Laborat'ry is the first that's been devised for the production of heavy water on any appreciable scale. And when I say 'appreciable scale' I'm speaking relatively; for Doctor Taylor told me last night that the daily output even at their plant is less than a cubic centimeter. But they're hopin' to step up production to about a teaspoonful a day. At present Princeton has on hand less than half a pint of this precious fluid. The cost of production is enormous; and because of the demand for samples of the liquid by scientists all over the country, the price asked for it is over a hundred dollars a cubic centimeter. A teaspoonful would cost over four hundred dollars, and a quart about a hundred thousand dollars. . . ."

He glanced up at Markham and continued.

"There are great commercial possibilities in this new commodity. Doctor Taylor tells me that already there is a chemical firm out west which has begun to market it." *

Markham was profoundly interested, and he did not once take his eyes from Vance.

"You think, then, this heavy water is the answer to Saturday night's poisonings?"

"It may be one of the answers," Vance returned slowly, "but I doubt if it is the final answer. Too many things militate against its giving us the entire explanation. To begin with, its cost is almost prohibitive, and there is too little of it available to account for the recurrent water motif in the Llewellyn case."

* As I write this record of the Casino murder case, I note, in a dispatch to *The New York Times,* that the Imperial Chemical Industries, an important British organization, have begun the commercial production of heavy water and hope in time to be able to supply it to chemists, physicists and physicians the world over, at about fifty dollars a teaspoonful.

"But what of its toxic effect on the human system?" Markham asked.

"Ah! Exactly. Unfortunately, no one knows what effects liberal quantities of heavy water, taken internally, would have upon a human being. Indeed, the very small amounts of heavy water obtainable have made experimentation in this direction practically impossible. One can only speculate. Professor Swingle, at Princeton, has proved that heavy water is lethal to small fresh-water fish like the *Lebistes reticulatus;* and the tadpole of the green frog and the flat-worm have been shown to survive but a short time when placed in heavy water. The growth of seedlings in heavy water is retarded or entirely suspended; and this inhibit'ry effect on the functioning of the life protoplasm has led some experimenters in San Francisco to the hypothesis that the indications of old age and senility are caused by the normal accumulation of heavy water in the body."

Vance smoked a moment and then added:

"However, I am not satisfied that these speculations have any direct bearing on our particular problem. On the other hand, I'm rather inclined to think, Markham, that we are *intended* to work along just those lines. In any event, they may lead us to the truth."

"Just what do you mean by that?" demanded Markham.

"I met and talked with one of Doctor Taylor's bright young assistants last night—a Mr. Martin Quayle—an expert chemist, conscientious and resourceful, and a great asset to the doctor's staff. Personally, however, I shouldn't care to trust him too far. He has an inordinately ambitious nature. . . ."

"What has this fellow Quayle to do with my question?" snapped Markham.

"Quayle, d' ye see, was a classmate of Bloodgood's. Two aspirin' young chemists. Very good friends. Everything *gemütlich*."

Markham studied Vance thoughtfully for a moment. Then he shook his head.

"I feel there's a vague connection somewhere in that information," he said; "but I still can't see what possible bearing it has on the problem we're trying to solve."

"Neither can I," Vance admitted cheerfully. "I merely put the fact forward in lieu of anything more definite."

Markham had suddenly become irritable. He struck the desk with his fist.

"That being the case," he grumbled, "what have you gained by your mysterious trip to Princeton?"

"I really don't know," Vance returned blandly. "I'll admit I'm frightfully disappointed. I had hoped for much more. But I'm not entirely disconsolate.

There's an elusive theme running through the water song, and I hope to know more about it tonight. I'm taking another trip this afternoon—into the country, this time. Behold these rustic togs in which I am incased. I'm countin' on the thought of Quayle to guide my gropin' footsteps."

Markham inspected Vance shrewdly for a brief time. Then he snorted and gave him a wry smile.

"The rigmarole of the Delphic oracle; the perfect fortune-telling manner; the crystal-gazer at work. I should be used to it by now. . . . So you're taking a jaunt into the country?"

"Yes," Vance murmured dulcetly. "Up Closter way——"

Markham leaped to his feet.

"What's that!" he fairly bellowed.

"Oh, my dear Markham, don't startle me so. You have far too much energy." Vance sighed. "I say, would you ask Swacker to find out what companies supply water and electric power to the domiciles in and around Closter?"

Markham spluttered and compressed his lips. Then he rang for his secretary and repeated Vance's request to him.

When Swacker had gone out again, Vance turned to Markham and continued.

"And when you get the names, will you write me a jolly sort of letter of introduction to the managers? I'm seekin' information——"

"What information?"

"If you must know," said Vance sweetly, "I wish to inquire into the amount of water and electricity consumed by a certain prominent citizen in the vicinity of Closter."

Markham sank back in his chair.

"Good God! Do you think that Kinkaid——?"

"My dear fellow!" Vance interrupted. "I'm not thinkin'. Too great an effort." He sighed elaborately and would say no more.

A few minutes later Swacker came in with the information that Closter and its environs were supplied by the Valley Stream Water Company and the Englewood Power and Light Company, both with offices in Englewood.

Markham dictated the letters Vance had asked for; and ten minutes later we were headed for Englewood, a few miles from Closter.

Englewood is only a short distance from New York, and, thanks to Vance's expert driving, we reached that flourishing little town in less than half an hour. Vance inquired the way to the offices of the Valley Stream Water Company and, once there, sent in his letter to the manager. We were received by a pleasant, serious man of about forty—a Mr. McCarty—in a small private office.

"What can I do for you, sir?" he asked, after shaking hands. "We will be glad to help in any way we can."

"I'm particularly interested," Vance told him, "in finding out how much water is consumed by a Mr. Richard Kinkaid, near Closter."

"That information is easily obtained." He went to a steel filing cabinet and, after a moment's search, took from it a small manila-colored meter-reading card. Returning to his desk, he glanced at the record and then raised his eyebrows in surprise.

"Ah, yes," he said, after a moment, as if suddenly remembering something. "I recall the circumstances now. . . . Mr. Kinkaid has a one-inch meter and uses a great quantity of water. His rate, in fact is based on the 40,000 to 400,000 cubic-feet-per-year schedule. . . ."

"And Mr. Kinkaid has nothing more than a moderate-sized hunting lodge," supplied Vance.

Mr. McCarty nodded.

"Yes, I realize that. The amount of water service used by Mr. Kinkaid is sufficient for a manufacturing plant. The large consumption was called to my attention over a year ago. I could not understand the figure, and of course I investigated. But I found that the customer was satisfied; and therefore we had no alternative but to continue the service."

"Tell me, Mr. McCarty," continued Vance; "is there any variation in the amount of water consumed by Mr. Kinkaid according to the time of year? That is, are his meter readings higher in the spring and summer months than in winter, when the lodge is closed?"

"No," the manager replied, his eyes still scanning the figures, "there is practically no variation. According to the card, as much water is consumed in the winter months as in the summer months."

At length he glanced up at Vance.

"Do you think we should look into the matter further?"

"Oh, no. No. I shouldn't look into it," Vance returned casually. "By the by, how long has this excessive consumption of water been going on?"

The manager looked down at the card again, turned it over, and scanned the figures on the reverse side.

"The water connections were installed over a year ago—in August, to be exact—and the heavy consumption began almost immediately."

Vance rose and extended his hand to the manager.

"Thank you very much, sir. That's really all I want to know. I appreciate your kindness."

From the offices of the Valley Stream Water Company, we went to the offices of the Englewood Power and Light Company, a few blocks away. Again Vance sent his letter in to the manager—a Mr. Browning— and once more we were received without delay. When Vance told him that he wished to check on Kinkaid's consumption of electric current, he gave Vance a curiously shrewd look.

"It is not our custom, you understand, sir, to give out information of this nature," he said in a dignified conservative manner. "But, in the circumstances, I feel justified in telling you that Mr. Kinkaid—who is well known hereabouts—arranged with me, over a year ago, for a sufficient capacity to properly meet his requirements—which, I may add, were far in excess of the usual demand in connection with a house or hunting lodge of that size. Negotiations were completed for a supply to meet the demand of five hundred kilowatts instead of the customary five kilowatts."

"Thank you for that information, sir." Vance offered a cigarette to Mr. Browning and took one himself. "But when Mr. Kinkaid arranged with you for this large supply of current, did he tell you for what purpose it was going to be used?"

"I naturally asked him that question," the manager returned, "and he explained merely that he required such a capacity for experimental purposes."

"You did not push the matter further?"

"Mr. Kinkaid informed me," the other replied, "that the experimental work which was to be done was of a more or less confidential nature; and my detailed interest in it naturally ended at that point. You appreciate the fact, of course, that our business, as well as our ideal, is to give the best possible service to the public."

"Your attitude, sir," returned Vance, with a slight inclination of the head, "is quite correct. I am most grateful to you for your confidence."

Mr. Browning rose.

"I'm sorry I can give you no more information—unless you would like to know the exact amount of power consumed."

"No, thank you," said Vance, starting for the door. "You've told me all that we need to know at present." And he took his departure.

When we were again in the car, Vance sat at the wheel for several minutes in indecisive abstraction. Then he took out his cigarette-case and, with great deliberation, lit another of his *Régies*.

"I think, Van," he said slowly, "we'll take a look at Kinkaid's retreat. I have a general idea where it is. If we go astray we can make inquiries."

He turned the car about and headed back toward the Hudson River. When we were again on route 9-W Vance turned north along the Palisades.

"There should be a narrow roadway somewhere within the next few miles, and there may be a sign to guide us," he said. "Keep your eye out. If we miss it we'll have to go to Closter and inquire our way from there."

But this was not necessary, for about two miles

farther on we came upon a rustic weather-beaten guide-post at the entrance to a tree-lined private driveway leading away from the river, which told us that Kinkaid's hunting lodge was somewhere beyond.

Turning into this roadway, we came almost immediately to a densely wooded stretch of country. We were now in Bergen County, somewhere between Closter township and the New York state line, near that section of New Jersey called Rockleigh. Following this private road for perhaps half a mile, we suddenly came to a clearing in the centre of which stood an old two-story stone cottage, such as might have been built originally as a private residence. There was a look of utter desolation about it. The windows had been boarded up and there was a general air of desuetude about the small front porch and the massive door which was the main entrance to the lodge. Behind the house, on the right, was a metal garage. Vance drove his car into the dense thicket on the left and got out.

"It looks a bit deserted—eh, what, Van?" he commented as we approached the front door.

He pulled the old-fashioned brass knob several times; but though we could hear the tinkling of a bell within, there was no answer to his summons.

"I'm afraid there's no one here," he said. "And I had passionately hoped to gain access. Let's see what the rear of the place holds in store for us."

We walked down the pathway to the north, but

instead of going directly to the back of the lodge, Vance continued on toward the garage. The door was slightly ajar, but on the latch hung a large padlock. Vance gave this padlock his careful attention and then glanced into the garage.

"Signs of recent life," he murmured. "There's no car, but there's neither dust nor rust on the lock. Moreover, there are marks of automobile tires on the roadway, as well as traces of fresh oil on this cement flooring. Conclusion: the inhabitant or inhabitants of the lodge have only recently departed. Destination and time of his, or their, return, problematical."

He looked up at the rear elevation of the lodge and smoked in speculative silence.

"I wonder, . . ." he murmured at length. "It might be done. I say, Van, do you feel in a house-breakin' mood?"

He approached the small screened porch at the back of the house and mounted the short flight of wooden steps that led to it. The door was not latched and we stepped into the porch. There was a door leading into the lodge, and beside it a small pantry window. Both, however, were locked.

"Wait here a minute," Vance directed; and he disappeared down the porch steps into the rear yard. A few moments later he returned with a chisel from the tool-box of his car. "I have always had a suppressed urge to be a burglar," he said. "Now let's see. . . ."

He worked the flat blade of the chisel between the

two small sections of the pantry window, and after a few minutes of manipulation, he succeeded in throwing the circular bolt which held them locked. Then, by inserting the chisel under the lower sash, he was able to raise it. There was an empty wooden box standing in a corner of the porch, and this Vance placed beneath the window. Standing on it, he managed, with considerable effort, to squeeze himself through the narrow opening; and a moment later I heard a heavy thump as he disappeared into the darkness inside. In another minute, however, his face appeared at the window.

"No damage done, Van," he announced. "Come along in. I'll help you through."

I pulled my hat over my ears and worked myself forward through the window. Vance took me under the shoulders and drew me into the narrow dark pantry.

"My word!" he sighed. "Burglary is far too strenuous an undertakin'. I was quite right in renouncin' the career. . . . Now we must look for the cellar door. I doubt if there will be anything to interest us on the main floors."

The cellar door was easily found. It led directly off the kitchen which was divided from the pantry by a swinging door. Vance led the way down the stairs, holding his pocket cigarette lighter before him.

"Oh, I say!" I heard his voice from the semi-darkness ahead. "That's a curious door for an innocent hunting lodge."

I was directly behind him now, at the foot of the stairs, and, looking over his shoulder, I saw through the flickering light of the cigarette lighter's tiny flame an enormous solid-oak door, comparatively new. There was neither door-knob nor lock, but where the knob would ordinarily have been was a large iron drop bolt. Vance lifted the heavy bolt and pushed the door inward. From the black depths beyond there came an acrid chemical odor and a continuous, insistent hum, as of motors; and far off in the blackness I could see several tiny shimmering blue streaks of flame, as of Bunsen burners.

Vance stepped through the doorway and fumbled around on the adjoining wall. Finally he found the electric switch. There was a click; and a brilliant illumination from a dozen or more suspended electric bulbs replaced the darkness.

An astonishing sight met my eyes. The stone cellar, though originally it must have been nearly sixty feet square, had been extended on two sides, so that we now found ourselves in an underground room at least a hundred feet wide and a hundred and twenty feet long. It was filled with rows of enormous tables covered with thousands of small circular glass jars. At the rear of the cellar was a series of electric generators; and on some of the tables and wide shelves about the walls were elaborate collections of bottles and intricate chemical paraphernalia.

Vance looked about him and moved here and there among the heavily laden tables.

"My word!" he murmured. "Doctor Taylor would be green with envy if he could see this laborat'ry. Amazin'! . . ."

He walked across the room to a series of tables whose apparatus was quite unlike the rest, and where I had seen the blue flames.

"Heavy water, Van," he explained, indicating several cone-shaped bottles at the end of a long series of tubes, valves and cells. "There must be over a quart of it here. Large-scale production, this. If it's pure, Kinkaid has a fortune in those bottles. . . . Do you see how it's made, Van? A fascinatin' process."

He looked over the apparatus closely.

"The method of production used here is the same as the one devised by the chemists at Princeton—the first one, by the by, of any real practical value. Electrolyte from commercial electrolytic cells is first distilled to remove the carbonate and hydroxide. Sodium hydroxide is added, and then the solution is electrolyzed in those cells."

He pointed to several tables far down the room, containing innumerable hydrometer jars which were cooled by immersion in large shallow tanks of running water.

"The electrodes, you can see, are bent twice at right-angles to form anode and cathode in the neighboring cells; and the potential of the direct current is supplied from those motor generators over there. It takes about three days to diminish the electrolyte to about twelve per cent of its original volume; and then this concentrated electrolyte is partially neutralized by bubbling carbon dioxide through it. After that it is distilled and added to another group of cells—those on that series of tables at the rear—containing water of the same grade but still with the original sodium hydroxide content. Three successive electrolyses are carried out, which result in water containing about two and a half per cent of the heavy hydrogen isotope. From this stage onward the hydrogen contains the heavy isotope which is recovered by the apparatus on these tables."

He waved his hand over the elaborate chemical array in front of which we were standing.

"The mixed electrolytic gas passes from those cells at the right through this spray trap, then through this T-tube which, you observe, is immersed in mercury to form a safety valve for releasing excessive pressure; and finally it flows out through that capillary glass nozzle where it burns as a flame."

Vance dropped his cigarette to the floor and crushed it out with his toe.

"And that is the final step, Van, in the production of the world's most expensive liquid. The water formed by the combustion is condensed in this inclined quartz tube———"

There came to us the sound of soft rapid footsteps on the cellar stairs. Vance swung suddenly about and rushed forward. But he was too late. The great oak door had been drawn violently shut, and almost simultaneously the heavy iron bolt was thrown into its socket with a metallic thud.

Above the din of the motors and the flow of the running water in the shallow tanks we could distinctly hear the angry but triumphant chuckle of some one on the stairs.

CHAPTER XIV

THE WHITE LABEL

(Monday, October 17; 3 p. m.)

Vance stood staring at the blank heavy door, a wry smile on his lips.

"'Pon my soul, Van!" he murmured. "And I abhor melodrama. Moreover, we've had no lunch—and it's three o'clock. Unpleasant but interestin' situation." He drew up a small deal chair and, sitting down despondently, smoked thoughtfully.

Suddenly every light in the cellar was extinguished, and we were left in a black chemical-laden darkness.

"Our turnkeys have thrown the main switch," Vance sighed. "Well, well. Can you bear it, Van? I'm deuced sorry to have involved you in this fantastic predicament. . . . But let us see if our captors are communicative."

He went to the door and rapped on it loudly several times with the back of his chair. Footsteps again descended the stairs, and a muffled, unidentifiable voice asked:

"Who are you—and what do you want here?"

"I regret that I am Mr. Vance," Vance called back. "And I'd jolly well like some *homard à la Turque* and a bottle of light *Chauvenet*."

"You're going to get something worse than that," came the muffled voice which, despite its faintness, was harsh and vindictive. "How many of you are there?"

"Only two," Vance told him. "Quite harmless. Tourists. Sightseers in the wilds of Jersey."

"Harmless burglars—that's good!" And the voice chuckled viciously. "Anyway, you'll be harmless when I finish with you. I'll be calling on you in a minute—as soon as I notify the State Troopers." And we could hear ascending footsteps on the stairs.

Vance beat on the door again with his chair.

"Just a moment," he called out.

"Well, what'll it be now?" The voice seemed farther away this time.

"Before you annoy the *gendarmes*," Vance said, "I may as well inform you that the New York police know exactly where I am and why I came here. Also, I have an appointment with District Attorney Markham at five o'clock, and if I do not put in an appearance, this hunting lodge will be the scene of a most thorough tour of inspection. . . . But don't let the fact upset you. I have much to meditate on for the next few hours." I could hear him replacing the chair and sitting down. Then, by the tiny flash of his cigarette lighter, I could see him lighting a fresh *Régie*.

There was a short silence followed by footsteps on the stairs and the low murmur of voices. In a few moments the lights in the cellar blazed forth again and the motors resumed their hum. Shortly afterward came the sound of the iron bolt being lifted; and the ponderous oak door swung slowly inward.

At the foot of the stairs stood Kinkaid. His face looked more like a mask than ever.

"I didn't know it was you, Mr. Vance," he said in an icy tone entirely without modulation, "or I should not have acted so inhospitably. I drove up and noticed that the pantry window had been forced open. I took it for granted there were burglars here, and when I saw lights in the cellar I ordered the door bolted."

"That's quite all right," Vance returned dulcetly. "My social error—not yours."

Kinkaid held the door open and stood to one side. We mounted the stairs to the kitchen, and Kinkaid led the way into the lounge room. Beside a massive table at one side stood a heavy-set man of about thirty-five, with flaming red hair and a sullen, serious face. He wore puttees, a canvas work suit, and a heavy gray flannel shirt.

"Mr. Arnheim," Kinkaid announced casually, by

way of introduction. "He's in charge of the laboratory that you've just been inspecting."

Vance turned to the man and bowed slightly.

"Ah! A classmate of Bloodgood's and Quayle's?"

Arnheim gave a slight start, and his eyes clouded.

"Well, what of it?" he grumbled roughly.

"That'll be all, Arnheim," said Kinkaid, and dis-
missed the man with a wave of the hand.

Arnheim walked back to the kitchen and we heard
him go down the steps to the cellar. Kinkaid sat down
and scrutinized Vance with his fish-like eyes.

"You appear fairly well acquainted with my affairs," he commented.

"Oh, no. No. Only the obvious facts," Vance assured him pleasantly. "I was seekin' more data when
you arrived."

"It's lucky for you," said Kinkaid, "that it turned
out as it did. Arnheim's a bad boy when it comes to
uninvited guests in the laboratory. I'm on my way to
Atlantic City for a few days and Arnheim drove over
to Closter to fetch me here."

Vance raised his eyebrows.

"Deuced queer route from New York to Atlantic
City, don't y' know."

Kinkaid's face hardened, and his eyes became mere
slits.

"It's not so damned queer," he retorted. "I wanted
to go over some business with Arnheim before leav-

ing, so I took the train to Closter and had him meet me there. He's driving me to Newark later to catch the seven o'clock train to Atlantic City. . . . Does that explain my itinerary satisfactorily?"

"After a fashion, yes." Vance nodded. "It might be. Quite logical when explained. Gettin' away from the turmoil of the wicked city for a while—eh, what?"

"Who the hell wouldn't—after what I've been through?" Kinkaid had modified his tone, and spoke almost petulantly. "I've shut down the Casino for a while, out of respect for Virginia." He sat upright in his chair and fixed Vance with a vicious look. "Believe it or not, sir; but I'd like to get my hands on the brute that killed her."

"Noble sentiment," Vance murmured non-committally. "Primitive but noble. By the by, her water carafe was empty when we arrived at the house Saturday night."

"So my nephew informed me. But what of it? No crime in drinking a glass of water, is there?"

"No," admitted Vance. "Nor in manufacturing heavy water. . . . Amazin' plant you have here."

"The finest plant in the world," asserted Kinkaid with obvious pride. "It was Bloodgood's idea. He saw the possibilities of commercializing heavy water, put it up to me, and I told him to go ahead—that I'd finance it. In another month or so we'll be ready to market it."

"Yes—quite. Most enterprisin' chappie, Mr. Bloodgood." Vance nodded, his eyes on Kinkaid in dreamy absorption. "So Bloodgood worked out the idea, went to Quayle in the Frick Laborat'ry and got all the necess'ry data and plans; then he looked up Arnheim and put him in charge of operations. Three ambitious young chemists—all good friends— reaching out, so to speak. Very neat."

Kinkaid smiled shrewdly.

"You seem to know as much about my enterprise as I do. Did Bloodgood tell you?"

"Oh, no." Vance shook his head. "He very dexterously avoided the subject. A bit too strenuous in his avoidance, though. Aroused my suspicions. I toddled down to Princeton last night Put various things together. Your hunting lodge was indicated. So I toddled out."

"Why are you so interested in my laboratory?" Kinkaid asked.

"The water motif, don't y' know. Far too much water bubblin' up here and there in this poisoning case."

Kinkaid sprang to his feet, and his face became an ugly red.

"What in hell do you mean by that?" he demanded thickly. "Heavy water isn't a poison."

"No one knows, don't y' know," returned Vance mildly. "It might be. No way of tellin' yet. Interestin' subject. . . . Anyway, water was indicated. I've simply been following the sign-posts."

Kinkaid was silent for some time. At length he nodded thoughtfully.

"Yes, I can see what you mean now." He shot Vance a penetrating glance. "Did you find out anything?"

"Nothing I hadn't suspected," Vance answered evasively.

"Too bad your housebreaking was without gratifying results."

"Housebreaking—oh, yes. To be sure." Vance shrugged. "Were you thinkin' of preferrin' charges?"

Kinkaid chuckled.

"No, I'll let it go this time." He spoke almost good-naturedly.

"Thanks awfully," Vance murmured, rising. "That being the case, I think Mr. Van Dine and I will stagger along. Sorry to appear in such haste, but I'm dashed hungry. No lunch, d' ye see." He went to the door and paused. "By the by, where will you be stayin' in Atlantic City?"

Kinkaid showed interest in the question.

"You think you may want to reach me?" he asked. "I'll be at the Ritz."

"A pleasant visit," returned Vance; and we went out to the car.

It was barely half-past four when we arrived home. Vance ordered tea and a change of clothes. Then he telephoned to Markham.

"I've had a jolly afternoon," he told the District Attorney. "Went housebreakin'. Got myself and Van locked in a dark cellar—same like a shillin' shocker. Mentioned your name. Open sesame. Was ceremoniously—not to say apologetically—released. Had a chat with Kinkaid. And here I am about to imbibe some of Currie's excellent *Taiwan*. . . . Kinkaid, by the by, is making quarts of heavy water at his Jersey hunting lodge. Large, elaborate plant. Bloodgood's idea—aided and abetted by another classmate, a gruff chappie named Arnheim. Kinkaid doesn't seem particularly annoyed that I uncovered his secret. Even forgave me for making forcible entry. He's headed just now for relaxation at Atlantic City. . . . The water trail progresses. I'm carryin' a bucket or two of cold water, figuratively speaking, to the Llewellyn domicile in a little while. . . . A queer case, Markham. But light is beginning to break. Not a blindin' illumination. Still, sufficiently bright to show me my way about. . . . Dinner at my humble diggin's at eight-thirty, what? . . . Then we'll hear the Brahms Third at Carnegie Hall. It's Rimsky-Korsakov the first half, and I'd infinitely prefer *canard Molière* and a *Château Haut-Brion*. . . . I'll pour forth all the news when I see you. . . .

And I say, Markham, bring along Hildebrandt's report, if it's ready. . . . Cheerio."

At about six o'clock Vance presented himself at the Llewellyn residence. The butler admitted us with frigid dignity. Apparently he was not surprised at our call.

"Whom do you wish to see, sir?"

"Who might be here, Smith?" Vance asked.

"Every one is here, sir, except Mr. Kinkaid," the butler informed him. "Mr. Bloodgood and Doctor Kane are also here. The gentlemen are in the drawing-room with Mr. Lynn, and the ladies are upstairs."

Lynn Llewellyn, evidently having heard us in the hall, appeared at the drawing-room door, and invited us in.

"I'm glad you've come, Mr. Vance." He still seemed peaked and depressed, but his manner was eagerly expectant. "Have you found out anything yet?"

Before Vance could answer, Bloodgood and Doctor Kane came forward to greet him; and, the amenities over, Vance sat down by the centre-table.

"I've found out a few things," he said to Llewellyn. Then he turned directly to Bloodgood. "I've just come from Closter. I visited the hunting lodge and had a chat with Kinkaid. Interestin' cellar at the lodge."

Llewellyn walked to the table and stood beside Vance.

"I've always suspected the old boy had good wines at the lodge," he complained. "But he's never asked me out to sample any of them."

Bloodgood's eyes were on Vance. He ignored Llewellyn's remarks.

"Did you meet any one else there?" he asked.

"Oh, yes," Vance told him. "Arnheim. Energetic chap. It was he who locked us in the cellar. Kinkaid's orders, of course. Very annoyin'." He leaned back and met Bloodgood's gaze. "I met another classmate of yours last night—Martin Quayle. I was paying a flying visit to Doctor Hugh Taylor. Also had a peep at the Frick Laborat'ry."

Bloodgood moved a step, but his eyes did not shift. After a moment he asked:

"Did you learn anything?"

"I learned a great deal about water," Vance returned, with a faint smile.

"And did you learn perhaps," asked Bloodgood, in a cold steady voice, "who is responsible for what happened here Saturday night?"

Vance inclined his head affirmatively and took a deep inhalation on his cigarette.

"Yes. I think I learned that, too."

Bloodgood frowned and rubbed his hand across his chin.

"What steps do you intend to take now?"

"My dear fellow!" Vance sighed reproachfully. "You know perfectly well I can take no steps. It's rather difficult to learn certain facts, don't y' know, but much more difficult to prove them. . . . Could you, by any chance, help us?"

Bloodgood leaned over angrily.

"No, damn it!" His words fairly exploded. "It's *your* problem."

"Oh, quite—quite." Vance spread his hands hopelessly. "A sad and complicated situation. . . ."

Doctor Kane, who had been listening intently, shook himself, as if out of a bad dream, and got to his feet.

"I must be running along," he announced, looking nervously at his wrist-watch. "Office hours at six, you know; and I've two uterine cases waiting for diathermy." He shook hands all round and went out hurriedly.

Bloodgood paid scant attention to the doctor's departure. His interest was still focussed on Vance.

"If you know who's guilty," he said quietly, "and can't prove it, perhaps you intend to drop the case?"

"No, no," returned Vance. "Persistency—my watchword. And perseverance. Never say die, and that sort of thing. 'God is with those who persevere.' Comfortin' thought. And 'the waters wear the stones,' as Job put it. Interestin' comment, that. Water

again, you observe. . . . The fact is, Mr. Bloodgood, I'll have sufficient proof before long. There's a
chemical report due from the official toxicologist
tonight. He's a clever man. I'll have something to
go on by tomorrow."

"And if there is no poison found?" asked Bloodgood.

"Better yet," Vance told him. "That'll simplify
matters. But I'm sure there'll be poison—somewhere.
Too much subtlety in this case. That's its weakness.
But I like extended decimals. So much easier to write
pi than hundreds of digits."

"I see what you mean." Bloodgood looked at his
watch, and rose. "You'll excuse me. I've a seven
o'clock train to catch to Atlantic City. Kinkaid
wants me there. He's making the train at Newark."
He bowed to us stiffly and went toward the hall.

At the door he stopped and turned.

"Any objection," he asked Vance, "to my telling
Kinkaid what you've said to me about knowing who
poisoned Virginia?"

Vance hesitated before answering. Then he said:

"No, none whatsoever. A good idea. Kinkaid's
entitled to know. And I say, you might add that
tomorrow will end the case."

Bloodgood caught his breath and stared at Vance.

"You're sure you want me to tell him that?"

"Oh—quite." Vance exhaled a series of smoke

rings. "I presume you, too, are stopping at the Ritz?"

Bloodgood did not answer for some time. Finally he said:

"Yes. I'll be there." And, turning on his heel, he went out quickly.

He had no more than disappeared when Lynn Llewellyn sprang up and clutched at Vance's arm excitedly. His eyes were glittering and he was shaking from head to foot.

"My God!" he panted. "You don't really think——"

Vance rose quickly and shook him off.

"Don't be hysterical," he said contemptuously. "Go and tell your mother and sister that I'd like to see them for a moment."

Llewellyn, abashed and shamefaced, muttered an apology, and went from the room. When he returned, a few minutes later, he informed Vance that the women were both in Amelia Llewellyn's room and that they would see him there.

Vance went immediately upstairs, where Mrs. Llewellyn and her daughter were waiting for him.

After a brief greeting Vance, keeping his eyes on Mrs. Llewellyn, said to them:

"I think it only fair to tell you ladies what I have already told the other persons concerned in this case. I believe I know who is responsible for this hideous situation. I know who poisoned your son, madam, and who put the poison in your carafe, from which Miss Llewellyn drank. And I also know who poisoned your daughter-in-law and wrote the suicide note. At the present moment I can do nothing about it, as I haven't the necess'ry legal proof. But I am hoping that by tomorrow I may have sufficient facts in hand to warrant my taking definite measures. My findings will cause both of you much agony; and I wish you to be prepared."

Both women remained silent, and Vance bowed unhappily and went quickly from the room. But, instead of returning directly to the main floor, he turned down the hall toward the room in which Virginia Llewellyn had died.

"I want to take one more look around, Van," he said to me, entering the bedroom. I followed him in, and he closed the door noiselessly.

For five minutes he walked about the room, looking meditatively at each item of furniture. He lingered over the dressing-table; he again inspected the books on the hanging shelves; he opened the drawer of the night-stand and inspected its contents; he tried the door of the passageway that led to Amelia Llewellyn's room; and finally he walked into the bathroom. He looked about him, sniffed the perfume in the atomizer, and then opened the small mirrored door of the medicine cabinet. He gazed inside for several minutes but touched nothing. At length he snapped the door shut and came back into the bedroom.

"There's nothing more to be learned here, Van," he announced. "Let's go home and wait for the dawn."

As we passed the drawing-room door, we could see Lynn Llewellyn sitting in a chair by the fireplace, his head in his hands. Either he did not hear us, or he was too stunned by Vance's recent statements to bother with the conventional courtesies of hospitality, for he made no sign that he was aware of the fact that we were leaving the house.

Markham arrived at Vance's apartment at half-past seven.

"I feel the need of a few rounds of cocktails before dinner," he remarked. "This case has been bothering me all day. And your cryptic phone call didn't exactly elevate my spirits. . . . Give me the whole story, Vance. Why and how did you come to be locked in a cellar? It sounds incredible."

"On the contr'ry, it was quite reasonable," Vance smiled. "Van and I were housebreakers. We used a chisel as a jimmy to effect our entry into Kinkaid's hunting lodge. Most lurid."

"Thank God you got back safely." Markham spoke lightly, but there was a troubled expression in his eyes as he looked at Vance. "My jurisdiction doesn't extend to Jersey, you know."

Vance rang for Currie and ordered dry Martinis with Beluga caviar *canapés* and a glass of *Dubonnet* for himself.

"If you must have cocktails, . . ." he sighed, and shrugged. "Forgive me if I don't partake."

While Markham and I were having our cocktails, Vance, sipping his *Dubonnet*, related in detail the events of that memorable day. When he had finished Markham shook his head in consternation.

"And where," he asked, "did it all lead you?"

"To the poisoner," said Vance. "But knowing your legalistic mind, I can't present you with the guilty person yet. You couldn't do a thing. A grand jury would only hand up a presentment chidin' you for being over-ambitious." He became serious. "By the by, any report from Hildebrandt?"

Markham nodded.

"Yes; but it's not final. He phoned me just before I left the office and told me he'd been working all day but hadn't found any traces of poison yet. He seemed rather worried, and said he was going to keep at it tonight. It seems he's analyzed the liver, kidneys and intestines without any indicative results; and he is going to work on the blood, lungs and brain. He's apparently extremely interested in the case."

"I'd hoped for something more tangible by this time," said Vance, rising and pacing up and down.

"I can't understand it," he murmured, his chin forward on his chest. "There should have been poison found, don't y' know. My whole theory is totterin', Markham. I've nothing else to go on."

He sat down again and smoked for a while in silence.

"I looked over Virginia Llewellyn's boudoir again today, hopin' to hit on something; but nothing had happened to point a guidin' finger, except that the medicine chest has righted itself artistically. It's now as it was when I first beheld it. Everything in place. Pattern balanced again. Composition quite correct."

"Did you discover what it was that upset your æsthetic sensibilities yesterday?" Markham put the question without much interest.

"Yes. Oh, yes. There was a spot missin' yesterday —a white square. Nothing more significant than a druggist's label on a tall blue bottle. A bottle of eyewash. Some one had evidently taken the bottle out, after I had first inspected the cabinet, and put it back with the label at the rear or to one side. So, instead of my seeing yesterday a compositional value of a tall blue bottle with a large white label, I saw merely the blank blue rectangle of the bottle. But today the white label on the bottle was to the front as originally."

"Very helpful," Markham commented ironically. "Does that, by any chance, come under the head of legal evidence?"

Before Markham had finished speaking Vance was on his feet.

"By Jove!" He tried to keep the eager excitement out of his voice. "That reversed label may be what I was hoping for when I asked you to withdraw the police from the Llewellyn house. I didn't know what might happen if every one there was relieved of supervision and restrictions. But I thought *something* might happen. And the change in the position of that bottle is the only thing that has happened. I wonder. . . ."

He swung about and went toward the telephone. A few moments later he was talking with Doctor Hildebrandt at the city's chemical laboratory in the morgue.

"Before trying anything else, doctor," he said, "make an analysis of the conjunctivæ, the lachrymal sacs, and the mucous membrane of the nose. Test for the belladonna group. It may save you further investigation. . . ."

CHAPTER XV

(Tuesday, October 18; 9:30 a. m.)

Vance arrived at the District Attorney's office at half-past nine the next morning. After the chamber music at Carnegie Hall the night before, Markham had gone directly home, and Vance had stayed up until long past midnight, reading sections here and there in various medical books. He had seemed nervous and expectant, and after a Scotch and soda I had gone to bed, leaving him in the library; but I was still awake when he turned in some two hours later. The events of the day had stimulated my mental processes, and it was nearly dawn when I fell asleep. At eight Vance awakened me and asked if I wished to participate in the activities he had planned for the day.

I got up at once and found him in excellent mood when I joined him in the library for breakfast.

"Something final and revealin' should happen today, Van," he greeted me cheerfully. "I'm countin' on the conjunctivæ and the psychology of fear. I've told every one connected with the case, with the ex-

245

ception of Kinkaid, all I know; and Bloodgood can
be relied upon to relay my remarks to him in his
seaside retreat. I'm hopin' that some of the seeds
sown by my comments fell into good ground and will
bring forth fruit, perchance an hundredfold—
though I'd be jolly well satisfied with the sixtyfold
or even the thirtyfold. . . . We're heading for
Markham's office as soon as you encompass those
poached eggs. I could bear seein' Hildebrandt's latest
report. . . ."

Markham had been in his office only a short time
when we arrived. He was studying a typewritten
sheet of paper, and did not rise when we entered.

"You guessed it," he informed Vance immediately.
"Hildebrandt's report was on my desk when I got in."

"Ah!"

"Conjunctivæ, lachrymal sacs and mucous membranes of the nose all saturated with belladonna. Also
belladonna in the blood. Hildebrandt says there's no
doubt now as to the cause of death."

"That's most interestin'," said Vance. "I was
reading last night of a case of death in a four-year-
old child by the instillation of belladonna in the
eyes."

"But that being the case," Markham objected,
"where does your heavy water fit in?"

"Oh, it fits in perfectly," Vance returned. "We
weren't supposed to learn of the belladonna in the

membrane of the eyelids and the anterior part of the eyeball. We were supposed to plunge into heavy water, head first, so to speak. The poisoner's toxicology was quite all right in an academic sense, but it didn't provide for all possible eventualities."

"I don't pretend," Markham retorted irritably, "to understand your cryptic remarks. Doctor Hildebrandt's report, however, is sufficiently definite, but it doesn't help us in the legal sense."

"No," admitted Vance. "Legally speaking, it makes the case more difficult. It could still be suicide, don't y' know. But it wasn't."

"And it is your theory," Markham asked, "that belladonna was also the poison taken by Lynn Llewellyn and his sister?"

"Oh, no." Vance shook his head emphatically. "That was something entirely different. And the distressin' part of the whole affair is that we have no proof of murderous intent in any of the three poisonings. But at least we know where we stand now, with that report of Hildebrandt's on the records. . . . Any other news, perchance?"

"Yes," nodded Markham. "A rather peculiar piece of news. I don't attach any particular importance to it, however. But the first thing this morning, before I got here, Kinkaid phoned from Atlantic City. Swacker spoke to him. He said he was called back to New York unexpectedly—some business at the Casino—and if I cared to meet him there, and bring you along, he thought he could give us some further information about the Llewellyn case."

Vance was deeply stirred by this information.

"Did he mention any specific time?"

"He told Swacker that he was going to be very busy all day, and said two o'clock would be most convenient for him."

"Did you, by any chance, call him back?"

"No. He informed Swacker he was taking a train immediately. And I didn't know where he was stopping, anyway. Moreover, I saw no necessity for phoning him; and, in any event, I wouldn't have done anything till I spoke to you. You seem to have some ideas about the case, which, I'll admit, have not suggested themselves to me. . . . What do you make of his invitation? Do you think it's likely he's handing out any vital information?"

"No, I don't think so." Vance lay back and, half closing his eyes, pondered the matter for several moments. "Queer situation. He's deuced casual about it. He may be just worried about my discovery of his heavy-water enterprise yesterday, and wants to set himself right in case we suspect anything. He can't be seriously upset, though, or he'd come here to your office, instead of risking our disappointing him at the Casino. . . ."

Vance sat up suddenly.

"By Jove!" he exclaimed. "There's another way of lookin' at it. Casual—yes. But too dashed casual. Same like the rest of the case. No one actin' rationally. Always too much or too little of everything. No balance."

He got to his feet and walked to the window. There was a perturbed look in his eyes, and a deep frown on his forehead.

"I've been hopin' for something to happen—expectin' it to happen. But this isn't it."

"What did you think might happen, Vance?" Markham asked, studying Vance's back with a troubled look.

"I don't know," Vance sighed. "But almost anything but this." He tapped out a nervous tattoo on the dingy window-pane.

"I rather thought we were in for something sudden and startling. But the prospect of chatting with Kinkaid at two o'clock doesn't especially thrill me. . . ."

He turned round quickly.

"My word, Markham! This *may* be exactly what I wanted." There was a flash of expectant fire in his eyes. "It *could* work out that way, don't y' know. I was lookin' for more subtleties. But it's too late for them now. I should have seen that. The case has reached the forthright stage. . . . I say, Markham, we'll keep that appointment."

"But, Vance——" Markham started to protest, but the other interrupted him hurriedly.

"No, no. We must go to the Casino and learn the truth." He took up his hat and coat. "Call by for me at half-past one."

He went toward the door and Markham looked after him questioningly.

"You're sure of your ground?"

Vance paused with one hand on the door-knob.

"Yes. I think so." I had rarely seen him so serious.

"And what are you doing till half-past one?" inquired Markham, with a dry, shrewd smile.

"My dear Markham! You have a most suspicious nature." Vance's manner changed suddenly and he smiled back at Markham with bland good-nature. "*Imprimis*, I'm going to do a bit of telephonin'. That annoyin' chore accomplished, I shall betake myself to 240 Centre Street and have a heart-to-heart talk with the doughty Sergeant Heath. Then I am going shoppin'; and later I shall pay a fleeting visit to the Llewellyn home. After that I shall drop in at Scarpotti's and have eggs *Eugénie*, an artichoke salad and——"

"Good-by!" snapped Markham. "I'll see you at one-thirty."

Vance left me outside the Criminal Courts Building and I went direct to his apartment where I busied myself with certain routine work which had been accumulating.

It was a little after one when Vance returned. He seemed abstracted and, I thought, in a state of mental and physical tension. He said very little, and did not once refer to the situation that I knew was uppermost in his mind. He walked up and down the library for perhaps ten minutes, smoking, and then went into the bedroom where I could hear him telephoning. I could not distinguish anything he said; but when he returned to the library he seemed in more cheerful spirits.

"Everything is going well, Van," he said, and sat down before his favorite Cézanne water-color. "If only this case works out half as well as that beautiful organization," he murmured. "I wonder. . . ."

Markham arrived at just half-past one.

"Here I am," he announced aggressively and with a show of irritation; "though I see no reason why we couldn't have had Kinkaid come to the office and tell us what's on his mind."

"Oh, there's a good reason," said Vance, regarding Markham affectionately. Then he looked away. "I hope there's a good reason. I'm not sure—really. But it's our only chance, and we must take it. There's a fiend at large."

Markham took a slow, deep breath.

"I think I know how you feel. Anyway, I'm here. Shouldn't we be starting?"

Vance hesitated.

"Suppose there's danger?"

"Never mind that." Markham spoke gruffly. "As I said, I'm here. Let's carry on."

"There's one thing I must warn you and Van against," Vance said. "Don't drink anything at the Casino—under any conditions."

We went down to the car, and fifteen minutes later we had turned into West 73rd Street and were headed toward Riverside Drive. Vance drew up directly in front of the Casino entrance, and we got out of the car and went up the stone steps leading to the glass-enclosed vestibule. Vance looked at his watch.

"Exactly one minute after two," he remarked. "In the circumstances, that might be called punctuality."

He pressed the small ivory bell-button at the side of the bronze door, and, taking out his cigarette-case, selected a *Régie* with great care and lighted it. In a few moments we could hear the lock being turned. Then the door swung inward, and we stepped into the semi-darkness of the reception hall.

I was a little surprised to see that it was Lynn Llewellyn who opened the door for us.

"My uncle was hoping you might come," he said after greeting us pleasantly. "He expects to be rather busy, and asked me to come over to help him. He's waiting in his office. Will you be so good as to come up?"

Vance murmured his thanks, and Llewellyn led the way toward the rear of the reception hall and up the wide stairway. He walked through the upper hallway into the Gold Room and, after knocking gently on Kinkaid's office door, he opened it and bowed us in.

I had barely become aware of the fact that Kinkaid was not in the office when the door slammed shut and the key was turned in the lock. I turned round apprehensively, and there, just inside the door, stood Llewellyn, slightly crouched, with a blue-steel revolver in his hand. He was moving the muzzle threateningly back and forth, keeping all three of us covered. A vicious change seemed to have come over the man. His eyes, half-closed but sinister and keen as daggers, sent a chill through me. His lips were contorted in a cruel smile. And there was a tense sureness in the poised swaying of his body, from which emanated the menace of some deadly power.

"Thank you for coming," he said in a low, steady voice, the sneer still on his lips. "And now, you dicks sit down in those three chairs against the wall. Before I send you all to hell I've got something to say to you. . . . And keep your hands in front of you."

Vance looked at the man curiously and then let his eyes rest on the revolver in his hand.

"There's nothing else to do, Markham," he said. "Mr. Llewellyn seems to be master of ceremonies here."

Vance was standing between Markham and me, and he resignedly seated himself in the middle chair. The three chairs had been placed in a row against the panels at one end of the office in obvious anticipation of our arrival. Markham and I sat down on either side of Vance and, following his example, placed our hands on the flat arms of the chairs. Llewellyn moved forward cautiously, like a cat, and stood about four feet in front of us.

"I'm sorry, Markham, for having got you into this," Vance murmured despondently. "And you, too, Van. But it's too late now for regrets."

"Spit out that cigarette," Llewellyn ordered, his eyes on Vance.

Vance obeyed, and Llewellyn crushed it out with his foot, without even glancing at the floor. "And don't make the slightest move," he went on. "I'd hate to have to drill you through before I tell you a few things."

"And we'd like to hear them, don't y' know," Vance said in a curiously suppressed voice. "I thought that I'd seen through all your system playing; but you're cleverer than I suspected."

Llewellyn chuckled softly.

"You didn't think far enough. You thought my

capital was exhausted—that I'd have to give up, a loser. But I still have six chips to play—these little steel chips here." He patted the cylinder of the revolver lovingly with his left hand. "And I'm placing two of them on each one of you. Does that play win?"

Vance nodded.

"Yes. It might. But at least you had to give up your subtleties in the end, and resort to direct methods. It wasn't, after all, the perfect crime. Only by turning gunman can you cover the bets you lost. Not an entirely satisfact'ry finale. A bit humiliatin', in fact, to one who regards himself as diabolically clever."

There was a devastating contempt in Vance's voice.

"You see, Markham," he added in an aside, "this is the gentleman who murdered his wife. But he wasn't quite clever enough to achieve his ultimate goal. His beautifully worked-out system went wrong somewhere."

"Oh, no," Llewellyn interjected. "It didn't go wrong. I merely have to carry the play a little further—one more turn of the wheel."

"One more turn." Vance smiled dryly. "Yes—quite. You will have to add three more murders to your scheme in order to cover the first."

"I won't mind that," said Llewellyn, with a vicious snarl. "In fact, it'll be a pleasure."

He stood, poised and alert, without the slightest trace of nervousness. The revolver in his hand was steady, and his gaze was cold and unfaltering. I watched him, fascinated. Everything about him seemed to personify swift and ineluctable death. The man possessed a power which seemed doubly terrible because of the soft, almost effeminate, contour of his features. There was an abnormal quality in him far more terrifying and sinister than the known and understandable terrors of life. He kept his eyes fixed on Vance; and after a moment he asked:

"Just how much do you know? I'll fill in the gaps for you. It will take less time that way."

"Yes, you would have to gratify your vanity," returned Vance. "I'd counted on that. A weakling at heart."

Llewellyn's lips twisted into a grim, evil smile.

"Do you think for one moment I haven't the nerve to shoot the three of you?" He tried to laugh, but only a harsh guttural sound issued from his throat.

"Oh, no. No." Vance spoke despondently. "I'm thoroughly convinced you intend to kill us. But that act will merely prove the desperation of your weakness. So simple to shoot people. The most illiterate and cowardly gangster is thoroughly proficient in that respect. It takes courage and intelligence to achieve one's end without the violence of direct physical action and, at the same time, to escape detection."

"I've outwitted all of you," Llewellyn boasted, in a hard, rasping tone. "And this little climax here is subtler than you think. I've a perfect alibi for this afternoon. If it interests you, I'm now driving through Westchester with my mother."

"Yes. Of course. I suspected something of the kind. Your mother was not at home when I went there this morning——"

"You were at the house this morning?"

"Yes. Dropped in for a moment. . . . Your mother would perjure herself for you, unfortunately. She has suspected you were guilty from the first, and has done everything she could to cover you and throw suspicion elsewhere. And your sister, too, had an inkling of the truth."

"That may, or may not, be," the man snarled. "Anyway, suspicions can't hurt anybody. It's proof that counts—and no one could prove anything."

Vance nodded.

"Yes. There's something in that. . . . By the by, you went to Atlantic City last night, didn't you?"

"Naturally. But no one knows I was there. I merely went to telephone on behalf of my dear uncle. That was simple enough; and it worked rather well, didn't it?"

"Yes. Apparently. Here we are, if that's what you mean. Lucky for your plan Mr. Markham's secret'ry doesn't know either your voice or Kinkaid's."

"That's why I was careful to phone before the eminent District Attorney had arrived at his office." He spoke with infinite sarcasm, and grinned exultantly.

Vance nodded slightly, his eyes still focused intently on the vicious-looking revolver now pointed straight at him.

"It's plain that you understood all I said to you at your home yesterday evening."

"That was easy," said Llewellyn. "I knew, when you were pretending to address your remarks to Bloodgood, that you were really talking to me, trying to tell me how much you knew. And you thought I'd be making some move soon to checkmate your knowledge, didn't you?" A sneer came and went on his lips. "Well, I did make a move, didn't I? I got you here—and I'm going to shoot you all. But that wasn't just the move you expected."

"No." Vance sighed unhappily. "I can't say that it was. The phone call and the appointment puzzled me considerably. I couldn't see why Kinkaid should have taken alarm. . . . But tell me, Llewellyn: how do you know this little party of yours is going to be a success? Some one in the building may hear the shots——"

"No!" Llewellyn, his deadly vigil unrelaxed,

smiled with shrewd self-satisfaction. "The Casino is closed indefinitely, and there's no one here. Kinkaid and Bloodgood are both away. I took a key to the place from Kinkaid's quarters at home weeks ago, thinking I might need it if he tried to hold up my winnings some time." Again he made a rasping noise in his throat. "We're entirely alone here, Vance, with no danger of interruption. The party will be a success—for me."

"I see you've thought things out pretty thoroughly," murmured Vance in a discouraged tone. "You seem to be in complete control of the situation. What are you waiting for?"

Llewellyn chuckled.

"I'm enjoying myself. And I'm interested in knowing just how much of my scheme you were able to figure out."

"It hurts you, doesn't it," returned Vance, "to think that any one should have seen through your plot?"

"No," snarled Llewellyn. "I'm just interested. I know you saw through some of it, and I'll tell you the rest before I put you away."

"That, of course, will come under the head of boasting," said Vance quietly. "It'll help build up your ego——"

"Never mind that!" Llewellyn's calm, cold tone was more terrifying than violent anger. "Tell your story—I want to hear it. And you'll tell it, too. As long as you can talk you're not dead—and every one likes to hang on to life, if only for a few more minutes. . . . And keep your hands on the arms of your chair—all three of you—or I'll shoot you to hell in a split second."

CHAPTER XVI

THE FINAL TRAGEDY

(Tuesday, October 18; 2:15 p. m.)

Vance looked at Llewellyn with critical tranquillity for several moments. Finally he spoke.

"Yes, you're quite right. As long as I continue to talk you'll let me live—since you feel I can feed your vanity. . . ."

"Vance!" Markham spoke for the first time since we had entered the Casino. "Why pander to this murderer? He's made up his mind, and there's apparently nothing to be done." His tone was husky and strained, but it held an undercurrent of courage and resignation which increased my admiration for him.

"You may be right, Markham," said Vance, his eyes gazing steadily at Llewellyn. "But there can be no harm in talking to our executioner before he pulls the trigger."

"Come on! Talk." Llewellyn spoke with exaggerated calm. "Or shall I tell the story myself?"

"No, that's not necess'ry—except for a few details here and there. . . . As I see it: you decided to get rid of your wife and to put the onus of the deed on

your uncle. Your wife was an encumbrance: both
you and your mother disliked her—and you'd feel
a little surer of a full inheritance if your wife was
out of the way. As for Kinkaid, you never liked him,
anyway; and, by eliminating him as a possible in-
heritor, you would be eliminating him also as another
source of irritation. You resent him passionately
because of his superiority to you and his open contempt for you. Quite the usual attitude of inferior
johnnies of your type. So you set to work, with your
vain, egotistic mind, to outline for yourself the perfect crime which would do away with all the factors
that stood in the way of your free functioning. And
you planned your coup, as you thought, so that,
whatever might happen, suspicion would point away
from yourself. . . . Clever idea. But you didn't
have the intelligence to perfect the plan."

Vance paused, his contemptuous eyes holding the
menacing gaze of Llewellyn. Then he went on:

"You conceived the idea of poison as the criminal
agent because it was indirect and underhand and
therefore obviated the need of courageous enterprise.
That is your nature, of course. You knew your wife
was using an eye-wash every night. And you'd read
in your father's books on toxicology—which you
probably consulted expressly for your purpose—that
it was possible to effect death through the absorption
of belladonna into the mucous membranes of the eyes

and nose. It was a simple enough matter for you to dissolve a quantity of belladonna or atropin tablets in the eye-wash. But you weren't sufficiently versed in modern toxicological methods—perhaps the fact that your father's books are not quite up-to-date was responsible for your ignorance—to know that today the stomach is not the only organ given to the analyst for examination. There used to be a mistaken idea that only an analysis of the stomach was necess'ry to prove or disprove a supposed poisoning; but in later books of research that point is gone into more thoroughly. You should have read Webster, or Ross, or Withaus and Becker, or Autenrieth. However, you did give us considerable trouble until my attention was attracted by the bottle of eye-wash in your bathroom medicine chest——"

"What's that?" Llewellyn's eyes opened a little wider, but their relentless vigilance did not relax. "You asked me about that medicine cabinet once."

"Oh, yes. At that time, though, I was merely gropin'. After you had taken the bottle of eye-wash and emptied it, Sunday morning, when you returned from the hospital, you put it back sideways, so that the label was not visible. I noted that something was wrong—though I didn't know just what. That's why we gave every one in your home perfect freedom of action all day Sunday. . . . By the by, you went to the pharmacist's Sunday—didn't you?—and had the

eye-wash bottle refilled with its original harmless solution, fearing an empty bottle might attract attention."

"I'll say yes. Go on."

"Thanks awfully for putting that bottle back with
the label to the front. That gave me the clue—and
the toxicologist's chemical analysis verified my
theory. I knew then that your wife had died from
the absorption of belladonna through the eyes and
that some one in the house had been manipulating the
eye-wash bottle to cover his tracks."

"All right, that's one step. And I suppose you
think Amelia and I were poisoned with belladonna,
too."

"No. Oh, no. Not belladonna. Even I know more
about toxicology than to think that. You poisoned
yourself with nitroglycerin."

Llewellyn's head jerked back a little.

"How did you know that?" he asked, scarcely
moving his lips.

"Simple deduction," Vance told him. "Doctor
Kane told me you had a bad heart and that he had
prescribed nitroglycerin tablets for you. You probably took one too many at some time, and it made
you a little groggy. So you looked up the action of
nitroglycerin and found that an overdose would
knock you out without doing you any lasting harm.
So, after setting the stage at home, you fed yourself

a good dose of the tablets and passed temporarily out of the picture, in full view of an audience. No way of ascertaining what the poison was, of course. Merely symptoms of collapse. I figured that was what you'd done the moment Kane told me of the nitroglycerin tablets."

"And Amelia?"

"The same thing. Only she was another unlooked-for development. You didn't intend the poison for her, don't y' know. You had planned that your mother should take the water from the carafe in which you had dissolved the nitroglycerin. But your sister upset your plans."

"You think I wanted to poison my mother?"

"Oh, no," said Vance. "Quite the contr'ry. You wanted her to appear as one of the victims of the plot—like yourself—so that she would be eliminated as a possible suspect."

"Yes!" A curious light shone in Llewellyn's eyes. "My mother had to be protected. I had to think of her as well as of myself. Too many people knew she didn't like my wife; and she is a hard, aggressive woman in many ways. She might have been suspected."

"That seems rather obvious," Vance returned. "And when you learned that your sister had taken the nitroglycerin, you tried another way to eliminate your mother from being suspected. When you heard us on the stairs Sunday morning, you enacted a touchin' Œdipus scene for our benefit, pretending you thought your mother might be guilty. A double subtlety. It tended further to eliminate you, and gave your mother the opportunity to convince us she was innocent. A bit cowardly, since it might actually have involved her. But effective—in a dramatic sense, of course. . . . Is there anything else you care to know regarding my conclusions?"

Llewellyn glowered maliciously for a moment; then he gave a barely perceptible nod.

"What did you think about the rhinitis tablets and the suicide note?"

"Just what you wanted me to think about them," Vance said. "They constituted one of the basic outlines of your plot. I'll admit it was well done. But I went a little farther than you intended me to go. You wanted me to accept Kinkaid as the reality; but I recognized him as your dummy victim."

Llewellyn frowned and his eyes narrowed dangerously. There was a colossal hatred in his expression. Then he grinned cunningly.

"So you saw through the suicide theory at once, did you?" he said. "Yes, that was what I intended. And was Kinkaid suggested to you immediately?"

"More or less," Vance admitted. "A bit too obvious, though."

"And the heavy water?"

"Oh, yes. That naturally followed, once I'd done a bit of figuring. As you intended. Your whole scheme was rather transparent as soon as one or two of the main factors had resolved themselves. The structure was well thought out, but some of the details were unconvincing. Lack of knowledge and research on your part, don't y' know. Quite childish, when added up. From the first I had you in mind as a possibility. . . ."

"You're lying," Llewellyn snarled. "Let's hear your reasoning."

Vance took a deep breath and shrugged his shoulders slightly.

"As you say, while I continue talking I remain this side of eternity. Ah, well, a few more moments. . . . In the circumstances I'm deuced grateful for the smallest favors. And I couldn't bear to depart this life leavin' you in a state of mental suspense."

His voice had become as cold and steady as Llewellyn's.

"Your letter to me, begging for my presence at the Casino Saturday night, was your first miscalculation. It was clever, however; but it was not quite clever enough. Obviously insincere—as was intended; but it said too much, revealin' more or less the character of the writer. A shrewd, tricky and effeminate brain conceived it, thereby indicatin' the type of person to look for. And really, y' know, it wasn't neces-

s'ry to have me witness your collapse at the Casino:
any one could have given me the details. But we'll
let that pass. . . . You typed that letter, as well
as the suicide note, rather badly, so as to indicate
some one unfamiliar with the machine—to wit: Kinkaid. You then posted the letter in Closter, to focus
attention on your uncle's hunting lodge near-by. But
that, too, was overdoing it; for if Kinkaid had actually sent the letter, he would have posted it anywhere
but in Closter. It's a minor point, however, and one
that I don't hold against you, for other things were
to transpire which would more than have counter-
acted so trivial an error. . . . The contents of the
rhinitis bottle were emptied to 'end a sort of left-
handed substantiation of Kinkaid's guilt. You knew,
of course, no belladonna would be found in the
stomach, and the fact would naturally point to a
spurious suicide. Your manipulation of the water
carafes was intended to give the impression that it
was through the medium of water that the poisons
had been administered. That, of course, was the
second sign-post—the Closter postmark being the
first—that led to the heavy-water motif. Once the
suicide theory had been exploded and the fact that
Kinkaid was manufacturing heavy water was discovered, suspicion against him would have been pretty
strong. And you and your mother would have been
automatically eliminated—provided she had taken

the nitroglycerin you prepared for her. . . . Am I correct in my reasoning thus far?"

"Yes," Llewellyn admitted grudgingly. "Go ahead."

"No one, of course," continued Vance, "knows what effect heavy water would have on human beings, if taken internally in large quantities, for there hasn't been enough of it available to make experiments along those lines, even if it were feasible to do so. But there has been considerable speculation as to the possible toxic effects of heavy water; and, while it could not have been proved scientifically that heavy water had been given you and your wife and your mother —had she drunk the water instead of your sister— there would have been a very powerful presumption of Kinkaid's guilt. And this presumption, taken with the other evidence you had fabricated, would have placed him in a predicament from which extrication would have been practically impossible. You knew, of course, that the nature of the poison supposed to have been given to you and your mother could not be determined because you would both have escaped its fatal effects. So your dear Uncle Richard was in for it. . . . By the by, how did you find out about Kinkaid's private enterprise at the hunting lodge?"

Llewellyn's eyes gleamed shrewdly.

"There's a fireplace running up from my room to

his, and I have often been able to hear him and Bloodgood talking up there."

"Ah!" Vance smiled disgustedly. "So you've
added eavesdropping to your other accomplishments!
You're not an admirable character, Llewellyn."

"At least I achieve my ends," the man retorted,
without the slightest show of shame.

"It appears that way. Perhaps I'm too critical.
But there's one thing I'll admit I don't understand.
Maybe you'll be so good as to enlighten me. Why
didn't you simply poison both your wife and Kinkaid
and save yourself the trouble of all these elaborate
subtleties?"

Llewellyn made a condescending grimace.

"That would not have been so easy to work out,—
Kinkaid's always on his guard. Moreover, his death
in addition to my wife's would have tended to cast
suspicion on me. Why take the chance? Anyway,
I'd rather sit around and watch him sweat. Ruin him
first—and then send him to the chair." A malicious
fanaticism shone in his eyes.

"Yes," nodded Vance. "I see your point. Playin'
safe and gettin' more satisfact'ry results. Very clev-
erly and subtly conceived. But we might not have
run upon the heavy-water idea, y' know."

"If you hadn't, I'd have helped you out. But I
counted on you. That's why I sent you the letter. I
knew the police would miss the heavy water; but I've

always admired the way your mind works in your investigations. You and I really have many qualities in common."

"I'm abominably flattered," murmured Vance. "And you did point up the water motif rather well, don't y' know. But Kinkaid and Bloodgood certainly played into your hands in the first act of your thrillin' drama here at the Casino."

Llewellyn chuckled.

"Didn't they? That was a stroke of luck. But it wouldn't have mattered. I'd already ordered plain water so you could hear me. And I was going to raise hell about the charged water if Bloodgood hadn't suddenly gone Chesterfieldian. You remember, too, that I waited until Kinkaid was standing near the table before ordering my second drink."

"Yes, I noticed that. Very clever. You played your cards well. Too bad you didn't read up on toxicology a little more."

"That doesn't matter now." Llewellyn snorted deprecatingly. "It's worked out better this way. Kinkaid will have three corpses right here in his office to explain away. He won't have a chance in the world, for even if he can prove an alibi he can't prove he didn't hire one of his henchmen to shoot you. And that's better than having him arrested on suspicion and tried on the circumstantial evidence of one poisoning on Park Avenue."

"So we, too, played into your hands," remarked Vance despondently.

"You did—beautifully." Llewellyn leered at Vance in triumph. "The cards are running for me these days. But luck and intelligence always go together."

"Oh, quite. . . . And when you have shot us you will join mother in the country to establish an unassailable alibi. Mr. Markham's secret'ry will testify that Kinkaid made an appointment with us here at two. You'll be able to give testimony about my talk with Bloodgood last night, and Kane will substantiate it. You'll also tell all you know of the heavy water, and Arnheim will have to admit I was at the hunting lodge. Our bodies will be found here; and since everything will point directly to Kinkaid, he'll be arrested and sent up." Vance nodded admiringly. "Yes. As you say. He hasn't a chance—whether it's eventually proved he did it himself or hired some one to do it for him. In any case, he's ruined. . . . Very pretty. I can't see a flaw in the reasoning."

"No." Llewellyn smiled. "I rather fancy it myself."

Markham was glaring at the man.

"You unspeakable fiend!" he blurted.

"Words, Mr. District Attorney—only words," the other returned in a tone of terrifying softness.

"Yes, Markham," said Vance. "Such epithets merely flatter the gentleman."

Llewellyn's lip curled hideously.

"Was there anything else you were in the dark about, Vance? I'd be glad to explain it."

"No." Vance shook his head. "I think the ground is pretty well ploughed up."

Llewellyn grinned with triumphant self-satisfaction.

"Well, I did it; and I got away with it. I planned everything from the start to the finish. I carried murder a little farther than it's ever been carried before. I supplied you with four suspects and kept well in the background myself. It didn't matter to me where you stopped. The farther you went, the farther you got from the truth. . . ."

"You forget we found you at last," Vance put in casually.

"But that's my greatest triumph," Llewellyn boasted. "I failed in a minor detail or two on my knowledge of poisons, and gave you a clue. But I met your suspicions with even a cleverer coup. I turned what you considered my defeat into one great culminating triumph." There was a maniacal gleam of egoism in his steady eyes. "And now we'll close the book!"

The muscles of his face relaxed into a cold, deadly

mask. There was an almost hypnotic glint in his pale blue eyes. He took a short step nearer to us, and with marked deliberation aimed with his revolver. The muzzle pointed directly at the pit of Vance's stomach. . . .

In any great final moment of this kind, in which all the life one has known is on the point of being wiped out, and when the thing called consciousness —to which we all cling with our innermost instincts —is about to be obliterated, it is curious how our minds receive and register the homely common sounds of the world about us—sounds that go unheeded in the ordinary course of events. As I sat there, in that terrible moment, I was aware that somewhere in the distance a woman's shrill voice was calling: I could hear the sound of a steam whistle on some boat in the Hudson: I was aware that, outside in the street, the brakes of an automobile had been violently thrown on: I was conscious of the low rumble of the traffic on the near-by avenue. . . .

Vance drew himself up a little in his chair and leaned forward. His eyes were narrowed and grim, but there was a contemptuous sneer on his lips. For a moment I thought he was preparing to leap up and grapple with Llewellyn. But if such had been his intention, he was too late. At that moment Llewellyn, his revolver still pointed steadily at Vance's stomach, pulled the trigger twice in rapid succession. There were two deafening detonations in the small office; and, accompanying them, two tongues of fire flashed from the muzzle of Llewellyn's revolver. A wave of horror passed over me and paralyzed every muscle in my body. . . . .

Vance's eyes closed slowly. One hand went to his mouth. He coughed chokingly. His hand fell to his lap. He seemed to go limp, and his head drooped. Then he pitched slowly forward on his face and lay in a distorted heap at Llewellyn's feet. My eyes, which felt as if they were bulging from their sockets, were focused on Vance in wild helpless horror.

Llewellyn glanced down at him quickly, without change of expression. He stepped a little to one side, at the same time taking precise aim at Markham, who sat as if petrified.

"Stand up!" Llewellyn ordered.

Markham took a deep audible breath and rose vigorously to his feet. His shoulders were squared defiantly, and not for a moment did his steady, aggressive gaze falter.

"You're only a policeman at heart," Llewellyn said. "I think I'll shoot you in the back. Turn around."

Markham did not move.

"Not for you, Llewellyn," he returned calmly. "I'll take anything you've got to give me facing you."

As he spoke I heard a curious unfamiliar sliding

noise at the other end of the little office, and I instinctively glanced in that direction. A startling sight met my eyes. One of the wide wooden panels in the opposite wall had apparently disappeared and in the opening stood Kinkaid, a large blue automatic in his hand. He was leaning slightly forward; and he held the gun at his hip pointed directly at Llewellyn.

Llewellyn also had heard the noise, for he turned partly and glanced suspiciously over his shoulder. Then there were two resounding explosions. But this time they came from Kinkaid's gun. Llewellyn stopped short in mid-movement. His eyes opened in glazed astonishment, and the revolver he held fell from his fingers. He stood as if frozen for perhaps two full seconds. Then all his muscles seemed to go limp: his head drooped, and he crumpled to the floor. Realizing what had happened, both Markham and I were too stunned to move or speak.

In the brief, terrible silence that followed, a startling and extraordinary thing happened. For a moment I felt as though I were witnessing some strange and uncanny bit of magic: a fantastic miracle seemed to be taking place. My fascinated gaze had followed Llewellyn's collapse, and my eyes had shifted to the still form of Vance. And then Vance moved and rose leisurely to his feet. Removing the handkerchief from his breast pocket, he began dusting himself.

"Thanks awfully, Kinkaid," he drawled. "You've

saved us a beastly lot of trouble. I heard your car drive up and tried to hold the johnnie off till you got upstairs. I was hopin' you'd hear the shots and would take a pop at him yourself. That's why I let him think he had killed me."

Kinkaid narrowed his eyes angrily. Then his expression changed, and he laughed gruffly.

"You wanted me to shoot him, did you? That's all right with me. Glad of the opportunity. . . . Sorry I didn't get here sooner. But the train was a little late, and my taxi was held up in traffic."

"Pray don't apologize," said Vance. "You arrived at exactly the right moment." He knelt down beside Llewellyn and ran his hand over the body. "He's quite dead. You got him through the heart. You're an excellent shot, Kinkaid."

"I always was," the other returned dryly.

Markham was still standing like a man in a daze. His face was pale, and there were large globules of perspiration on his forehead. He managed now to speak.

"You're—you're sure you're all right, Vance?"

"Oh, quite." Vance smiled. "Never better. I'll have to die some time, alas! But, really, I wouldn't let a pathological degenerate like Llewellyn choose the time for my demise." His eyes turned to Markham contritely. "I'm deuced sorry to have caused you and Van all this agitation. But I had to get Llewellyn's confession on the records. We didn't have any overwhelming evidence against him, don't y' know."

"But—but——" Markham stammered, still apparently unable to accept the astonishing situation.

"Oh, Llewellyn's revolver had nothing but blank cartridges in it," Vance explained. "I saw to that this morning when I visited the Llewellyn domicile."

"You knew what he was going to do?" Markham looked at Vance incredulously and rubbed his handkerchief vigorously over his face.

"I suspected it," said Vance, lighting a cigarette.

Markham sank back into his chair, like an exhausted man.

"I'll get some brandy," Kinkaid announced. "We can all stand a drink." And he went out through the door which led to the bar.

Markham's eyes were still on Vance, but they had lost their startled look.

"What did you mean just now," he asked, "when you said you had to get Llewellyn's confession on the records?"

"Just that," Vance returned. "And that reminds me. I'd better disconnect the dictaphone now."

He went to a small picture hanging over Kinkaid's desk and took it down, revealing a small metal disk.

"That's all, boys," he said, apparently addressing

the wall. Then he severed the two wires attached to the disk.

"You see, Markham," he elucidated, "when you told me this morning of the supposed telephone call from Kinkaid I couldn't understand it. But it soon came to me that it was not Kinkaid at all who had phoned, but Llewellyn. It was from Llewellyn that I was expecting some move, after the remarks I had poured indirectly into his ear last night. I'll admit I wasn't expecting anything quite as forthright and final as this little act: that's why I was puzzled at first. But once the idea dawned on me, I could see that it was both a logical and subtle move. Premise: you and I were in the way. Conclusion: you and I would have to be put out of the way. And, inasmuch as we were being lured to the Casino, it was not particularly difficult to follow Llewellyn's syllogism. I was pretty sure he had actually gone to Atlantic City to make the telephone call—it's difficult, don't y' know, to simulate a long-distance call from a local station. Therefore, I knew I had several hours in which to make arrangements. I called Kinkaid at Atlantic City at once, told him all the circumstances, and asked him to come immediately to New York. I also found out from him how I could get into the Casino to install a dictaphone. That's why I called on the doughty Sergeant. He and some of the boys from the Homicide Bureau and a stenographer are in an apartment of the house next door, and have taken down everything that has been said here this afternoon."

He sat down in a chair facing Markham and drew deeply on his cigarette.

"I'll admit," he went on, "that I wasn't quite sure what method Llewellyn would use to put us out of his way and throw suspicion on his loving uncle. So I warned you and Van not to drink anything,—there was, of course, the possibility that he would use poison again. But I thought that he *might* use his revolver; and so I purchased a box of blanks, went to his home this morning on a perfectly silly pretext, and when I was alone in his bedroom I substituted the blanks for the cartridges in his revolver. There was the chance that he would have noticed this substitution if he examined the gun from the front; but I saw that the blanks were in place before I took my seat beside you a while ago. Otherwise I would have practised a bit of jiu-jitsu on the johnnie immediately. . . ."

Kinkaid reentered the office with a bottle of brandy and four glasses. Setting the tray on his desk, he filled the glasses and waved his hand toward them, inviting us to help ourselves.

"Shall I, Vance?" Markham asked, with a grim smile. "You told us not to drink anything here."

"It's quite all right now." Vance sipped his *Cour-*

voisier. "From the very first I have regarded Mr. Kinkaid as our most valuable ally."

"The hell you say!" Kinkaid grumbled good-naturedly. "After all you put me through!"

At this moment there came to us the sound of a slamming door, followed by heavy, hurrying footsteps on the stairs. Kinkaid stepped to the office door leading into the Gold Room, and opened it. On the threshold stood Heath, a Colt revolver in his hand. Behind him, crowding forward, were Snitkin, Hennessey and Burke. Heath's eyes, fixed on Vance, were wide in childlike amazement.

"You're not dead!" he almost shouted.

"Far from it, Sergeant," Vance returned. "But please put away that gun. Let's not have any more shootin' today."

Heath's hand dropped to his side, but his astonished eyes did not leave Vance's face.

"I know, Mr. Vance," he said, "you told me that I wasn't to get upset at anything I heard over the dictaphone, and to stay on the job till you gave me the sign-off. But when I heard what that baby said, and then the shots and you falling, I beat it right over."

"It was sweet of you," returned Vance. "But unnecess'ry." He waved his hand toward the limp figure of Lynn Llewellyn. "There's the chappie. No trouble. Shot through the heart. Quite dead. You'll have to get him to the morgue, of course. But that'll

be that. Everything worked out beautifully. No
pother. No trial. No jury. Justice triumphant nevertheless. Life goes on. But why?"

I doubt if Heath heard anything Vance said. He
continued to stare open-mouthed.

"You're sure—you're not hurt?" The words
seemed to come from his lips in an automatic expression of his apprehension.

Vance set down his cognac glass and, going to
Heath, put his hand affectionately on the other's
shoulder.

"Quite sure," he said softly. Then he wagged his
head in mock commiseration. "Frightfully sorry to
disappoint you, Sergeant."

.   .   .   .   .

The murder of Virginia Llewellyn, as you perhaps
remember, occupied the front pages of the country's
press for several days, but it soon gave way to other
scandals. Most of the major facts of the case became
public property. But not all of them. Kinkaid was,
of course, exonerated for the shooting of Lynn Llewellyn: Markham saw to it that the affair was not even
brought before the Grand Jury.

The Casino was permanently closed within a year,
and the beautiful old gray-stone house was torn down
to make way for the construction of a modern sky-
scraper. By that time Kinkaid had amassed a small

fortune; and the manufacture of heavy water has occupied him ever since.

Mrs. Llewellyn recovered from the shock of her son's death in far shorter time than I had thought possible. She threw herself more energetically than ever into social-welfare work, and I see her name frequently in the papers in connection with her philanthropic activities. Bloodgood and Amelia Llewellyn were married the week after Kinkaid had closed the doors of the Casino for all time, and they are now living in Paris. (Mrs. Bloodgood, incidentally, has given up her artistic career.) I met Doctor Kane on Park Avenue recently. He had an air of great importance, and informed me he was rushing to his office to give a woman patient a diathermic treatment.